‖‖‖‖‖‖‖‖‖‖‖‖‖‖‖‖‖‖‖‖‖‖‖

W9-AZP-069

What am I going to do with John?

As she stared out the window of the airplane at the clouds below, the question echoed in Sydney's mind.

I'm going to get hurt. I can tell myself that I can handle anything that comes along, that I'm only in this relationship for the pleasure it gives me now, that I can walk away from him without regrets, but I no longer know if that's true.

What was going to happen to her when John finally realized that the two of them were on different tracks? That her goals were incompatible with his?

How was she going to handle it when he dumped her?

She closed her eyes. There was no answer to the last question that didn't make her feel sick inside.

Because the unthinkable had happened.

She had fallen in love with him.

Dear Reader,

Welcome to Silhouette **Special Edition**...welcome to romance.

Some of your favorite authors are prepared to create a veritable feast of romance for you as we enter the sometimes-hectic holiday season.

Our THAT SPECIAL WOMAN! title for November is *Mail Order Cowboy* by Patricia Coughlin. Feisty and determined Allie Halston finds she has a weakness for a certain cowboy as she strives to tame her own parcel of the open West.

We stay in the West for A RANCHING FAMILY, a new series from Victoria Pade. The Heller siblings—Linc, Beth and Jackson—have a reputation for lassoing the unlikeliest of hearts. This month, meet Linc Heller in *Cowboy's Kin*. Continuing in November is Lisa Jackson's LOVE LETTERS. In *B Is For Baby*, we discover sometimes all it takes is a letter of love to rebuild the past.

Also in store this month are *When Morning Comes* by Christine Flynn, *Let's Make It Legal* by Trisha Alexander, and *The Greatest Gift of All* by Penny Richards. Penny has long been part of the Silhouette family as Bay Matthews, and now writes under her own name.

I hope you enjoy this book, and all of the stories to come. Happy Thanksgiving Day—all of us at Silhouette would like to wish you a happy holiday season!

Sincerely,

Tara Gavin
Senior Editor

Please address questions and book requests to:
Silhouette Reader Service
U.S.: 3010 Walden Ave., P.O. Box 1325, Buffalo, NY 14269
Canadian: P.O. Box 609, Fort Erie, Ont. L2A 5X3

TRISHA ALEXANDER
LET'S MAKE IT LEGAL

Silhouette®

SPECIAL EDITION®

Published by Silhouette Books
America's Publisher of Contemporary Romance

If you purchased this book without a cover you should be aware that this book is stolen property. It was reported as "unsold and destroyed" to the publisher, and neither the author nor the publisher has received any payment for this "stripped book."

For three terrific friends: Julie Kistler and Jeanne Triner, who are great role models and gave me something to shoot for with Sydney; and Alaina Richardson, who provided so much background material and help with this book.

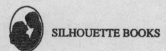 SILHOUETTE BOOKS

ISBN 0-373-09924-X

LET'S MAKE IT LEGAL

Copyright © 1994 by Patricia A. Kay

All rights reserved. Except for use in any review, the reproduction or utilization of this work in whole or in part in any form by any electronic, mechanical or other means, now known or hereafter invented, including xerography, photocopying and recording, or in any information storage or retrieval system, is forbidden without the written permission of the editorial office, Silhouette Books, 300 East 42nd Street, New York, NY 10017 U.S.A.

All characters in this book have no existence outside the imagination of the author and have no relation whatsoever to anyone bearing the same name or names. They are not even distantly inspired by any individual known or unknown to the author, and all incidents are pure invention.

This edition published by arrangement with Harlequin Enterprises B.V.

® and TM are trademarks of Harlequin Enterprises B.V., used under license. Trademarks indicated with ® are registered in the United States Patent and Trademark Office, the Canadian Trade Marks Office and in other countries.

Printed in U.S.A.

Books by Trisha Alexander

Silhouette Special Edition

Cinderella Girl #640
When Somebody Loves You #748
When Somebody Needs You #784
Mother of the Groom #801
When Somebody Wants You #822
Here Comes the Groom #845
Say You Love Me #875
What Will the Children Think? #906
Let's Make It Legal #924

TRISHA ALEXANDER

has had a lifelong love affair with books and has always wanted to be a writer. She also loves cats, movies, the ocean, music, Broadway shows, cooking, traveling, being with her family and friends, Cajun food, *Calvin and Hobbes* and getting mail. Trisha and her husband have three grown children and two adorable grandchildren and live in Houston, Texas. Trisha loves to hear from readers. You can write to her at P.O. Box 441608, Houston, TX 77244-1603.

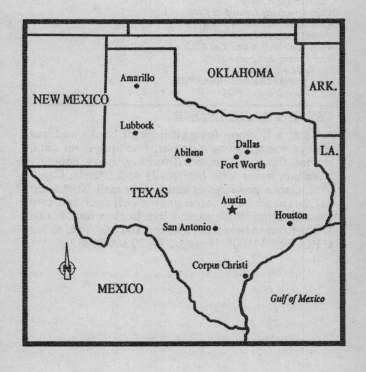

Chapter One

"You'll *have* to go, John. There isn't anyone else we can send."

John Appleton stared at his twin sister, Janet, his partner at Appleton Legal Temps. "You're not serious."

"I'm deadly serious. What else can we do?"

"There's got to be someone else," John insisted.

Janet shook her head. "There isn't. Come on, John, you can do it. After all, you used to be a lawyer."

"They aren't asking for a lawyer. They're asking for a paralegal."

"Yes, I know, but they'll be getting a bargain and won't know it." Janet sighed and pushed her mop of dark curls away from her face. Her normally cheerful expression had been replaced with a worried look. "We sweated blood to snag Folger & Hubbard, and you know their biggest concern when they signed with our agency was whether or not we'd be able to keep up with their demand, especially during emergencies. If we tell them our last available paralegal came down with the flu, they'll call another agency. And then we might lose them permanently. Are you prepared to take that chance?"

John knew Janet was right. Their agency was only eighteen months old and still not as solidly grounded in the Houston legal community as they'd like it to be. The two of them had worked their butts off to build the business they now had, and losing their most valuable client would be a blow they didn't need. Sometimes he wondered why he'd ever thought going into the legal temporary business was a good idea.

He heaved a sigh. "Damn. I guess I don't have a choice."

Janet's expression relaxed. "Who knows? You might even enjoy yourself."

John grimaced. "I wouldn't go that far. But it ought to be interesting—working for The Shark." The Shark was one of the nicer names their temps had assigned to Sydney Scott Wells, one of Folger & Hubbard's fast-track lawyers and the agency's most exacting and hard-to-please client.

Janet frowned again. "I just hope she doesn't get upset about this. You'll be particularly nice to her, won't you, John?"

"I'll be so nice our own mother wouldn't know me." He removed his suit jacket from the closet and put it on. "You'd better call her secretary and explain about the substitution. And you'd also better explain that I'm going to be late." He glanced up at the wall clock, which read 8:05. Jo Whipple, the temp who had called in sick, was supposed to report to work at Folger & Hubbard at eight o'clock, but John figured he'd be lucky to make it by eight-thirty. "Oh, and what about the kids? Can you pick them up after school?"

"Yes, yes, yes, don't worry," Janet said. "I'll take care of everything. You just keep Sydney Wells happy."

Sydney Scott Wells tapped her gold pen against the glass-topped surface of her desk. Honestly! Of all times for Gerri to get sick, this week was the worst. Sydney was buried up to her eyeballs in work and had planned to spend the day in the War Room with her team. There were a million things to do to get ready for the Montgomery case, which was set for trial on Monday.

She rubbed her temples. She didn't have time to hold hands with a new paralegal who wouldn't know where anything was, who wouldn't be familiar with her cases and who probably wouldn't be one-third as good as Gerri, anyway.

Sydney eyed the stack of files on her desk—a stack that seemed to grow taller by the hour. She was already putting in twelve- to fourteen-hour days, six days a week, and it looked as if she'd have to increase her hours if she wanted to have a prayer of keeping up with her caseload.

She grimaced. She had hoped to be able to get away for a couple of days now that the weather had finally cooled off. It was late October, her favorite time of the year, and she'd thought about going to San Antonio to visit her best friend from law school days. She sighed heavily. She'd have to scratch that idea, she guessed, at least until this trial was over.

For a moment, Sydney considered passing a couple of her less important cases off to one of the younger attorneys, but as quickly as the thought formed, she dismissed it. As tempting as it was to lighten her own load, she couldn't do that.

The kids depended on her. They trusted her, and many of them had never been able to trust an adult before. Most of them had been betrayed by adults all of their lives. She could not betray them, too.

She massaged her forehead. She was just tired, that's all. And disgruntled because this was the third time in as many weeks that Gerri had had to go home sick.

Sydney sighed again, then punched her intercom. "Norma, come in here."

Less than a minute later, her secretary rushed into Sydney's office. "Hasn't that temp gotten here yet?" Sydney demanded.

Norma winced as if Sydney had struck her. "N-no, not yet."

Sydney wasn't sure which exasperated her more: her secretary's scared-rabbit expression or the tardiness of the temp. "Didn't you tell that agency when you called them yesterday afternoon that whoever they sent today needed to be here at eight o'clock sharp?'' she said crossly.

''Yes, of course I did,'' Norma answered, her voice strained. ''M-maybe she got lost.''

''Lost? Gee, if she can't even find the building, that certainly bodes well for the day, doesn't it?'' Sydney expelled a noisy sigh. ''Gawd! Couldn't they send us someone who's at least *been* here before?''

''It was such short notice, Miss Wells....'' Norma pleated her skirt in a nervous gesture that added fuel to Sydney's irritation. ''She'll be here. Temps are often late their first day.'' Norma's voice gathered strength as she seemed to muster her courage. ''Sometimes they misjudge how long it'll take to get somewhere new.''

''What's her name, anyway?''

''Uh, Jo Whipple.''

''Well, send her in the minute she shows up,'' Sydney said, resisting the impulse to add her observation that if Jo Whipple didn't have the good sense to check out where she was going and how to get there in advance of the assignment, Sydney didn't have high hopes for her ability to do the work that needed doing.

Instead, she rooted through the files littering her desk until she found the one she wanted and began reading. When she glanced up again, Norma was gone.

Twenty minutes later, the temp had still not been shown into Sydney's office. Sydney threw down her pen and after glaring into space for a minute, got up and marched outside to Norma's cubicle.

Norma stood talking to a tall, dark-haired man in a well-cut gray suit. She was smiling in that way women smiled when the man paying attention to them was good-looking or sexy or both. "I'm glad you finally got here," she was saying, her green eyes all bright and shiny. "Miss Wells has been waiting—"

"Norma!" Sydney snapped. Norma jumped. The man turned around.

"Th-this is the new paralegal," Norma stammered. "Joe Whipple. Mr. Whipple, this is Miss Wells. You'll be working for her today."

She'd been right, Sydney thought. He *was* good-looking. Sexy, too, with a long, lean face and high-bridged nose. He had intelligent brown eyes that met her gaze squarely and without a flicker of apology for his tardiness.

He extended his hand, the beginnings of a smile hovering around his well-shaped mouth. "Hello, Miss Wells. Actually, I'm not J—"

"You're late." She ignored his hand and gave him her frostiest glare. Did he think she'd be bowled over by his charm, thereby excusing his tardiness?

The smile faded. "Yes, I know, and I'm sorry, but I—"

"I don't care to hear your excuses. We've got too much work waiting to be done to waste time with excuses."

His eyes hardened, and now they *did* flicker, but not with apology, and Sydney knew he was angry. Well, wasn't that too bad? For a moment, she thought he was going to say something else—she almost wished he *would* say something else—because she still had anger to vent, but he must have thought better of it, because he simply looked at her.

"I go to trial on Monday," she added. "We're using seventeen experts. What I want you to do today is call each expert and make sure they're prepared. They'll have to be on call all week."

"Fine."

Sydney turned to Norma. "Norma, have you finished the Carlson brief yet?"

"It's printing now, Miss Wells." Norma's eyes were wary as she looked first at Sydney, then at Joe Whipple.

"Good. Bring it in as soon as it's ready. Come with me, Mr. Whipple." Sydney strode into her office. She could hear him following her. "Shut the door behind you."

Without glancing back, she walked to her desk. A stack of files sat on one end. "Those are the files you're going to work with today." She walked behind her desk and sat down. "Have a seat. We'll go over them, then I'll show you where you're going to work."

"All right," he said. He lifted the stack of files, then sat opposite her. His brown eyes met hers.

"How much experience do you have, Mr. Whipple? Or do you prefer to be called Joe?"

Something glinted in the backs of his eyes. "I have over fourteen years' legal experience. And I prefer to be called John."

Sydney frowned. "I thought Norma said your name was Joe."

"Yes, she did, but I've been called John all my life."

Sydney shrugged. It was no skin off her nose if he wanted to be called John. As long as he could do the work, she didn't much care what his name was. "Fine. Now, shall we get started?" She picked up a legal pad and handed it to him. "You'd better take notes."

He took the pad and removed a pen from the inside pocket of his suit jacket. He settled back in his chair.

"Have you heard or read anything about Kara Montgomery?" she asked.

Raising his eyebrows, he said, "You mean the little girl who wants to divorce her birth mother?"

Sydney nodded.

"Yes, of course, I've heard of her. Is that *your* case?"

"Yes. As you can imagine, with a case of this magnitude, I want very much to win. But that's not the only reason this is so important to me. Kara is a special child and I care about her. I believe she has a right to be happy and secure. Unfortunately, children's rights have been abused and ignored for far too long."

For the first time since John Whipple had arrived, there was an approving gleam in his eyes as he nodded his agreement. Sydney felt some of her irritation evaporate as she began to fill him in on the details.

Kara Montgomery was ten years old, and like the boy in the precedent-setting Florida case, had been a ward of the state of Texas for nearly eight of those years. Her birth mother—Shanna Montgomery—had never been able to care for her, and her father was unknown.

For the first two years of her life, Kara lived with her grandmother, but then her grandmother died, and she'd been in several foster homes ever since. For the past four years, she'd lived with the same foster parents and during that time had had little to no contact with Shanna. Her foster parents, George and Lottie McKinsey, were an older couple who adored her and wanted to adopt her.

At first, Shanna Montgomery had given her permission for the adoption, but then she'd changed her mind. She was getting married again, and she wanted Kara back. Kara did not want to go back. She loved the McKinseys and wanted to live with them forever. The McKinseys were ordinary people who didn't have a lot of money, but when they came to Sydney and asked her to take the case, she didn't hesitate.

The case would not earn the firm much money, but that didn't really matter. Winning a high-profile case such as this one would bring recognition and prestige to Folger & Hubbard. It would also bring many more clients—clients who *would* earn the firm a lot of money. The senior partners had been in complete agreement when they approved Sydney's request to represent Kara.

"All right, now let's go over the experts," Sydney said when she'd finished briefing him. "The first one—it should be the top folder—is Dr. Alan Hawthorne, the state psychiatrist who did the initial evaluation of Kara. He will testify that, in his opinion, removing Kara from the first stable home she's ever had would be extremely damaging to the child."

For the next twenty minutes, Sydney gave John the background on each expert. When they'd covered all seventeen, she said, "Now you're clear on what I want you to do today?"

"I think so. I'm to call each witness, be sure they know when they're supposed to go, double-check that their exhibits are in order, remind them of relevant portions of their depositions, make sure they've got everything straight as far as where they're staying, et cetera."

He sounded confident enough, she thought. "Any questions?"

"Not yet."

"You're sure?"

"Positive."

Sydney had to admit she was impressed by his knowledgeable, businesslike attitude. Perhaps the day would turn out to be less of a disaster than she'd first thought. "Fine. Then let me show you to your desk."

Throughout the rest of the morning, as Sydney and her team worked in the War Room, she would periodically walk down the hall to check on John. Each time she approached his desk, he was either on the phone with a witness or quietly marking a file.

Each time, he would look up and smile. He seemed to be doing just fine. There was no need for her to worry.

She finally relaxed and concentrated on her own work.

By noon John regretted his impulsive decision not to inform Sydney Wells of his true identity. He wasn't sure exactly what his thought processes had been when he'd gone along with the false information conveyed by her secretary.

He guessed he'd had some kind of idea of getting back at Sydney for her rudeness. He smiled ruefully. Yeah, he'd been ticked off by the way she talked to him, and he'd thought it would serve her right to string her along, but now he knew it had been a stupid thing to do.

He wished he could tell her the truth.

Unfortunately, it was too late for that. She would be furious with him for deceiving her, and he couldn't blame her for that. In her place, he'd be furious, too. It didn't matter that she'd behaved badly. She was obviously under a lot of pressure and feeling the stress. He could see that she was not only overworked, but a high achiever. A person who placed impossibly high standards on herself and expected others to live up to them, too.

She reminded him of the way he used to be.

Of the way Andrea used to be.

The thought of Andrea—of what he'd lost when he lost her—threatened to mire him in sadness and those almost overwhelming feelings of grief and loss that had just about done him in that first year after her death.

John gave himself a mental shake. Grief was self-indulgent. It was a luxury he could no longer afford. Not if he hoped to build a happy life for his children—one that made them feel safe and loved and secure. He had vowed, after Andrea died, that he would put Emily and Jeffrey first. That he would no longer spend the majority of his time concentrating on his career and making money. Andrea's death had shown him that the time he spent with the people he loved was more important than anything else.

That's why he'd given up his law career.

That's why he was working in an office in his home—so he could be there for his children.

That's why he found himself here today working for Sydney Wells.

It amazed him that he'd had no idea this woman his employees referred to as The Shark was a passionate children's advocate. True, he had lost touch with the movers and shakers of the legal community and didn't keep up with who was representing whom, but you'd think he'd have heard *something* about Sydney Wells's specialization.

This fact alone was enough to earn his grudging admiration, even though he had a feeling her tough exterior was a facade she effected, probably because she was a female in a male-dominated profession.

He grinned to himself. Sydney Wells had certainly done everything in her power to turn attention away from her femininity. Today—and John was sure today was no exception—everything she wore was designed to blend in with her male colleagues: severely cut gray suit that fell midcalf, plain white blouse, utilitarian black watch, low-heeled black pumps, hardly any makeup. Even her hands, which were slender and well-shaped, were unadorned, and the nails were filed to a medium length and unpolished.

But all her attempts to deemphasize her gender hadn't worked. Each time she walked into the vicinity of his desk, he was very much aware of her as a female. An attractive female. Even that scowl that appeared much too often couldn't detract from her appeal.

He watched her walk away—back toward the conference room that had been designated as the War Room. She was tall. He guessed about five foot nine or ten. Andrea had been tall, too. John smiled, remembering how at one time he'd thought he liked his women tiny. Andrea had changed that misconception. Andrea had changed a lot of things in his life. Sydney had nice legs, too, he thought, wishing he could see more of them. He wondered what she'd look like in a short, colorful dress—something that would bring out the brilliant blue of her eyes and the honey-blond highlights of her hair.

He shook himself. Better get back to work. Sydney Scott Wells wasn't paying him to daydream.

At three o'clock, Sydney left the War Room and headed toward her office. She beckoned to John to come inside. "I've got a couple of other calls I want you to make."

They had just sat down when there was a knock on the door. "Come in," Sydney called.

Doug Farrell, like herself one of the newer partners, opened the door and poked his head inside.

Sydney suppressed a groan when she saw him. She couldn't stand Doug, not only because he was the type of person who would cut your throat if he thought it would further his career, but because he was one of the most conceited, chauvinistic men she'd ever met.

The phrase "He thinks he's God's gift to women" had probably been coined with Doug in mind. He hated her because she'd brushed off every overture he'd ever made in her direction and because she made no secret of her disdain for his behavior.

"Hey, Sydney," he said, strutting in with what Sydney secretly termed his peacock walk, "thought I'd find you here." He looked curiously at John, who glanced up and met his gaze. "Who's that?" he said, cocking his head toward John.

"A temporary paralegal, filling in for Gerri," Sydney said curtly, not that it was any of his business. "What can I do for you, Doug?"

Doug's grin expanded. "There are lots of things you could do for me, Sydney, baby, and you'd probably enjoy them all if you'd just loosen up and let yourself go for a change." He winked at John.

Sydney counted to ten and drummed her fingers on her desk top. "I've heard this all before," she said through gritted teeth, "so could we skip the comedy routine?"

"Hey," he said innocently, "can't you take a joke? That's what's wrong with women like you. You have no sense of humor at all." He gave John a conspiratorial smile.

"Just what is it that you wanted, Doug?" Sydney avoided John's eyes. Bad enough she had to put up with a sleeze like Doug, but to have John witness his baiting and her impotence in the face of it was humiliating.

"I need you to take a depo for me at four o'clock. Gotta witness coming in and I'm scheduled to tee off with Oscar Farrington at four-fifteen."

Sydney seethed inside. "Look, despite what you might think, I actually have something important to do for the rest of the afternoon." Under her breath, she muttered, "Unlike you."

His handsome face hardened. "Golfing with clients is important. All you have to do is look at how much business I bring to the firm to know that."

Sydney sighed. "Yes, yes, I know. You're wonderful."

"Are you always this much of a bitch, Sydney?" Doug snarled. "Or is it that time of the month?"

Sydney slammed her hand down on her desk. She could feel her face heating and knew she probably looked like a lobster. "I could bring you up on charges if you keep making those kinds of remarks, Doug."

His eyes widened. "I don't know what you're talking about."

"You know exactly what I'm talking about."

"I only meant *because you're in the middle of billing time...*"

Sydney stared at him. "Find someone else to do your work," she said.

"Up yours," was his parting remark. Then he slammed out of her office.

Sydney's heart was beating too fast. She looked at John. "I suppose you think I'm a bitch, too."

"No, actually, I was thinking something entirely different."

Sydney felt oddly flustered by the expression in his dark eyes.

He smiled. "I was thinking, if I were you, I'd have been tempted to punch that creep right in the middle of his costly nose job!"

Something soft and sweet slid into Sydney's stomach as John Whipple's warm brown eyes met hers, his gaze admiring and entirely without censure.

She shrugged. "I'm used to Doug. Unfortunately, he's not the only one around here who thinks the way he does. He's just the most obnoxious and blatant." She couldn't help the note of bitterness that had crept into her voice. "The others talk behind my back."

"Don't pay any attention to them. They feel threatened. The only way a lot of guys know how to relate to a strong, aggressive female is to put her down. Before my wife died, she ran into the same kind of thing with some of the lawyers she dealt with—" He broke off, grimacing. "Sorry. I'm talking too much."

Sydney finished giving him her instructions, then he left to go back to his desk. She bent her head to her work, but she couldn't stop thinking about John Whipple.

What was a man like him doing working as a temp? He was obviously well-educated, and he was certainly presentable and attractive. He'd said his wife was dead. Wonder what happened? She must have died awfully young, because Sydney was sure John was still in his thirties. And he'd said his wife had dealt with lawyers. Had she been a paralegal, too? *Dealt with,* he'd said. Not *worked for.*

For the next two hours, curiosity about her temporary paralegal kept Sydney from concentrating as hard as she needed to. When the small clock on her desk chimed the hour, she realized it was five o'clock and time for John to leave for the day. She got up and walked out to his cubicle. He was closing the files and stacking them neatly. He'd put on his suit coat again.

"I might need you again on Monday," she said. "If I do, I'll call the agency."

He looked up quickly. "They might have another assignment for me."

Sydney knew that Folger & Hubbard was Appleton Legal Temps biggest client. If she wanted John Whipple again, she'd get him. But all she did was nod. "Were you able to reach all the experts?"

"All but Reba Morrison, but her sister said she'd be back in town on Sunday and that she was ready for the trial."

"Good. Is there something I have to sign before you leave?"

He gave her a look of chagrin. "I forgot to bring a time sheet. I'll mail it to you."

"All right."

He stuck out his right hand. She took it. As his warm hand enfolded hers, shaking it firmly, she was once again consumed with curiosity.

"I enjoyed working with you today," he said, smiling.

Sydney smiled, too. "Sorry I was so rude this morning. I was just—"

"No apologies necessary." He released her hand. "Good luck with the case. I'll be watching your progress in the newspapers."

"Thanks."

He turned to go, and Sydney suddenly had to ask him the question that had bothered her for most of the day. "John . . ."

He turned, his eyebrows raised in question.

"Can I ask you something?" she said.

"Sure."

"What's a man like you doing working as a temp?"

He looked at her for a long moment, then said, "It's hard to explain. Let's just say circumstances dictated it."

Sydney couldn't have said why his answer didn't sit right, but long after he'd left the office, she was still convinced that he had been evasive.

The question was why?

Chapter Two

"So how did things go today?" Janet asked before John even got the door shut behind him.

"Do you want to hear the good part first or the bad part first?" John countered, grinning.

Janet clapped her hand over her mouth. "Oh, no. What happened that was bad?"

John removed his suit coat and loosened his tie. "Before I tell you about it, tell me why you never called Sydney Wells's secretary to tell her I was coming instead of Jo Whipple."

"I tried, John. But she was away from her desk the first time I called, and then she was on another line and I couldn't wait because I had a call, and before I knew it, it was already nine o'clock, and I figured by then you would've gotten there and they'd know about the substitution, anyway." Janet made a face. "Sorry. Did it make things uncomfortable for you?"

"You could say that." John proceeded to tell her how Sydney's secretary had thought he was Jo Whipple. "Before I could correct her, she'd already introduced me to her boss, and The Shark nearly bit my head off about being late. She said she had no time for excuses. She ticked me off," he admitted, not proud of the way he'd allowed himself to lose his professionalism, "so I let her go on thinking I was Jo Whipple."

"You *what?*" Janet exclaimed, eyes wide. "Oh, John. Why did you *do* that? What's she going to think if she ever finds out? Somehow, I don't think she's the type who takes kindly to being deceived."

John grimaced. He knew Janet was right. Although Sydney Wells had shown her vulnerable side to him today, she would be furious over his dishonesty, which would probably negate all of the positive feelings he knew they'd shared by the end of the day.

"Yeah, well, by the time I'd decided I shouldn't have gone along with the misconception, no matter *what* she said to me, it was too late to correct it without making things even worse. But she'll never find out."

Janet's forehead remained creased in a worried frown. "Aside from that, how did the day go?"

"The work was a piece of cake."

"What about Sydney Wells? Is she as bad as everyone says she is?"

"I didn't think she was so bad. She's driven and aggressive—you know the type—a typical over-achiever."

"So you got along with her all right?"

"Yeah, I did. In fact, I found myself sympathizing with her at one point. I also have to admit, I ended up admiring her. She's got guts."

"Really?"

"Yeah. She crossed swords with a hotshot colleague. You know, one of those jerks you run into a lot in some of these firms. He tried to embarrass her in front of me. But she held her own. In fact, she got in some pretty good digs."

"You almost sound as if you *liked* her," Janet commented.

John smiled. "I did. She...she reminded me of Andrea." He was immediately sorry he'd added the last bit of information, for his sister's face slid into astonishment.

"Andrea! Oh, John, come on. From everything our temps have said, Sydney Scott Wells is *nothing* like Andrea."

"They were wrong." Even though John wished he'd kept his mouth shut, he felt a strange sense of loyalty to Sydney.

Janet gave him a look that said she didn't believe him.

"I think I knew Andrea better than anyone else, Janet," he reminded her.

"Yes...well..." But Janet didn't look convinced. "What made you think she's like Andrea? Does she look like her?"

"No. She's blond and blue-eyed." Andrea had been the stereotypical redhead—green-eyed and freckled. "But she's tall like Andrea was. And she's also sharp, very sharp. And smart." Those were also characteristics of Andrea's, as Janet very well knew.

"But Andrea was so friendly and so nice," Janet said.

"Sure. Around you. But she had another side to her in her professional world. She had to. Nice, agreeable women don't get very far in the legal business. Nice, agreeable women don't get very far in *any* business. You should know that, Jan."

"Well, why do you think our temps are so afraid of Sydney Wells if she's as great as you seem to think she is?"

"Probably because she's tough. She drives her secretary and everyone else relentlessly, including herself." John chuckled. "She's also short on tact at times."

"She doesn't sound like someone *I'd* like," Janet said. "I'll bet she's hard-looking."

"No," John said, thinking how he'd felt Sydney was anything but hard-looking.

"Did you think she was attractive?"

John shrugged. Suddenly, he didn't want to discuss Sydney Scott Wells any longer. "Yeah, I guess so." He looked around. "Where are the kids?"

"Mom called and invited Emily to go shopping for her birthday, and Jeffrey's over at Benjamin's house."

John nodded. His six-year-old son and Benjamin Newberry were best friends, especially since Benjamin's dad had built him a treehouse.

"Mom said she and Emily would eat at the mall, so not to expect her home until about eight-thirty." Janet stood. "I guess I'll be going. Mike and I are going out for Chinese tonight. Do you and Jeffrey want to come with us? We'd love to have you."

"Thanks, but I don't think so. We've got some leftovers. We'll manage."

John liked his brother-in-law, Mike Cameron, but he wasn't in the mood to go out to eat, even though he knew Jeffrey loved eating out. He'd take both kids out tomorrow night, instead.

"Oh, and Mom also invited all of us for Sunday dinner."

"What, Cecelia Appleton is going to cook?" John grinned. "What's the occasion?"

Their mother never cooked. She hated to cook. And since their father had died several years earlier, she had given up even the pretense of cooking. She'd once told John that she considered cooking in the same category as cleaning toilets.

Janet laughed. "I think she's feeling guilty. Like she's fallen down on the job of being a mother."

"What time are we supposed to be there?"

"Two o'clock." Janet picked up her purse. "John, what are we going to do if Sydney Wells ever finds out who you really are?"

John walked over and put his hands on his twin's shoulders. He leaned down and kissed her cheek. "Let's not borrow trouble, okay?" He turned her around and gave her a little push toward the door. "Now quit worrying, and go home. We'll see you Sunday."

* * *

"Well, Sydney, I wasn't sure if you'd show up to-day." Helena Wells's dark blue eyes always seemed judgmental to Sydney. Always seemed to say her youngest daughter wasn't measuring up. Again.

To cover the feelings of inadequacy and frustration prolonged exposure to her mother and sisters always produced, Sydney shrugged. "I always try to make Sunday dinner if I can."

Her mother smiled. "I know. I'm glad you're here. It's too pretty a day to spend cooped up in the office."

Sydney nodded. It *was* a gorgeous day—cool, with low humidity—the first really crisp fall day Houston had seen after a long, hot summer that had had even the hardiest natives complaining.

As Sydney followed her mother through the house and into the enormous family room that overlooked the pool and backyard, she saw that her three sisters and their families were already there, gathered around the television set watching the Oilers game. As Sydney walked in, a loud cheer erupted as the Oilers made a successful play.

Claire, her oldest sister at forty-two, smiled when she saw Sydney. She immediately got up from the couch and walked over, extending her arms for a hug. As they embraced, Sydney felt a swift rush of love. Besides their father, Claire was the only one in Sydney's family she felt close to.

"We missed you last week," Claire said as they drew apart.

Sydney smiled, then looked around at the rest of the family.

"Hey, Syd," said Tom Stevens, Claire's husband. He grinned up at her from his spot on the floor, his freckled face reflecting his good nature.

Sydney liked Tom. Who could help liking him? He was like a puppy—he lived to please—but sometimes she wondered how Claire, who was witty and intelligent, could stand being married to him. Sydney often wondered what the two of them talked about. Or didn't people talk after they were married? She thought about her own parents, whose conversation seemed to consist of discussions about their children and what they would eat for dinner.

Eliza waved from the kitchen, and Sydney gave a little wave back. Sydney and Eliza couldn't stand each other, but by unspoken agreement they pretended to be sisterly in front of their parents.

The two had absolutely nothing in common. Eliza, at thirty-nine, was the antithesis of Sydney. Sydney often thought that the only important thing in Eliza's life was how she looked and what men thought of her.

As far as Sydney could tell, once Eliza was out of school, she'd never again opened a book, never thought about a social issue and never had any ambition except to be married to a rich man.

She had attained her goal. At twenty-six, she'd married Driscoll Worth, whose name lived up to its promise. He was worth millions, and when he and Eliza had divorced two years ago, Sydney's sister had acquired several of those millions.

Eliza had custody of their daughter, Carolyn, who was ten. Sometimes Sydney worried about Carolyn, who had a curious mind and showed signs of a social conscience. It couldn't be good for a child like her to live with a mother like Eliza.

Still, who was Sydney to judge? She didn't have children.

Sydney looked around for her niece, but Carolyn wasn't there today. Her gaze met that of her third sister, Wendy. Only two years separated the two, but like Sydney and Eliza, she and Wendy had nothing in common.

"Hi," Wendy said from her seat in the recliner.

"Hi," Sydney responded. "How're you feeling?" Wendy was seven months pregnant with her fourth child.

"Okay."

Sydney nodded. As always, she felt awkward talking to Wendy, who never offered anything to keep the conversational ball rolling. "Where are the kids?"

"They got bored with the game so Dad took them outside."

Sydney had wondered where her father was. The two of them had always been very close. Sid Wells was a man's man, and he had always wanted a son. When his fourth daughter was born, he'd taken one look and decided she would be the son he'd never had. So he'd insisted on naming her Sydney and he'd raised her to do all the things men do. As a result, Sydney felt confident in the competitive business arena and completely inadequate in the more feminine social sphere.

"Hey, Sydney, do you want something to drink?" asked Wendy's husband, Craig, who stood at the bar.

"Some ginger ale?" Sydney walked over to the bentwood rocker in the corner and sat down. She eyed the TV set. She hated football.

Craig brought her the ginger ale she'd requested, and Sydney took a sip.

"Geez! Would you look at that?" moaned Tom. "Three missed tackles!" He made a gesture of disgust. "Why do I watch football, anyway?"

"Because it's so much *fun*," Craig said sarcastically.

"Because hope springs eternal," Eliza said.

Because men love games, Sydney thought.

Just then, the back door opened, and Wendy's three, ranging in age from nine to two, erupted into the room, followed more slowly by Sydney's father. He saw her immediately and his face lit up. She got up and walked over to him. They hugged.

"How's the case coming?" he asked as he released her. "You ready for tomorrow?"

"Almost. I'm going back to the office after dinner to look everything over one last time."

"Not much will happen tomorrow," her father predicted. "Just the voir dire." Sid Wells had had his own successful law practice before he'd retired two years earlier. He had once told Sydney that the day she decided to become a lawyer was the proudest day of his life.

"I know," Sydney said, "but I want to be sure I haven't overlooked anything."

"You haven't. My girl is always prepared. You're going to set this town on its ear when you win that case. You mark my words."

Sydney smiled weakly. She knew her father loved her, but sometimes the weight of his pride and expectations were suffocating. As soon as the disloyal thought formed, she pushed it away.

What did she want him to do? Act as if he doubted her abilities? Of course not. Of course he was proud of her. Of course he expected great things of her. And she wouldn't let him down.

During dinner, the talk once more turned to Sydney's case. This time Claire said, "I'm thinking of coming down to watch the trial, Sydney, but it'll probably be a zoo, won't it?"

Sydney nodded, pleased that her sister cared enough to want to be there. "Unfortunately, I'm afraid so." With the publicity this case had generated, she knew the media would be out in full force, as would the curious.

"That's okay," Claire said. "I'll come, anyway."

"Don't say *unfortunately*," her father boomed from his end of the table. "You want all the publicity you can get, Sydney. This case is going to make your name a household word."

"I'm not sure I want to be a household word," Sydney said.

"Oh, sure you do," Craig interjected. "Why else do you take on these cases? They sure don't bring your firm any money."

Sydney gave him a sharp look. Was that a bit of a snide taunt she heard in his tone? Wendy's husband was a lawyer, too. But his area of expertise was patent law, an area Sydney considered dull. Sydney had often wondered if he was jealous of her high-profile cases. "I take them on because I believe in these cases," she said quietly. "Making a lot of money has never been important to me."

"She doesn't need to worry about money," Sid Wells said. "Not now. Not when she's building her reputation." He beamed at Sydney. "She's smart. She's taking her time. She knows what's important in the long run."

Craig's face reddened. "Some of us don't have that luxury. Some of us have three, almost four kids to raise—"

"Who wants dessert?" Sydney's mother, always the peacemaker, interjected smoothly. "It's pineapple upside-down cake."

"My favorite," said Tom, who always moved in to reinforce his mother-in-law's efforts when it came to avoiding any kind of scene. He patted his stomach expectantly.

The women, except for Wendy, all stood and began clearing the table.

"I don't think I'll stay for dessert, Mom," Sydney said, carrying her dishes out to the kitchen. "I'm edgy about tomorrow, so I'm going back to the office."

"All right, dear," Helena said. "Do you want to take a piece of cake with you?"

"No, thanks." Sydney put the dishes down and leaned over to kiss her mother's soft cheek. As always, her mother smelled of White Linen, her favorite perfume. "I'll try to come next Sunday, but I may not make it. Once this trial starts, I'm going to be really busy."

"I know. Good luck. I'll be thinking of you."

As Sydney drove toward her downtown office, she wondered just exactly what her mother would be thinking. She knew her mother's greatest wish was that Sydney marry and have a family as her sisters had. Yet there had been times when Helena actually seemed to understand what Sydney was trying to accomplish, when she actually seemed proud of her youngest daughter.

Sydney had long ago resigned herself to the fact that she wasn't ever going to marry or have children. And it was best that way, she knew. Marriage was hard enough without having to contend with the female partner's demanding and obsessive career.

There had been a time when Sydney had—like most other young girls—dreamed of marriage, but she'd never met a man who had interested her enough for her to want to spend the rest of her life with him. She intimidated most men, and she accepted that.

She sighed. Enough of that. She needed to empty her mind of everything but the Montgomery case. She felt confident of her ability in the courtroom, and she wasn't really worried, but still…you never knew when something might go wrong.

The worst thing that could happen to an attorney during a trial was to be hit with a surprise, which was always a possibility. No matter how you prepared, no matter what contingency you anticipated, sometimes things happened, like a jury hating a witness, or information surfacing that you didn't expect. That's when things went wrong, when even a sympathetic jury could turn on you.

Sydney wasn't really afraid of this. She and Gerri and the two younger lawyers who would assist Sydney had done their research thoroughly.

Gerri. God, Sydney hoped Gerri showed up in the morning. Still, if she didn't, Sydney at least had an alternative. She would call the Appleton agency immediately and ask for John.

Sydney smiled, thinking of John Whipple. She had really enjoyed having him work for her on Friday. Actually, she wouldn't mind having him come in again. Not in preference over Gerri, of course, but she had to admit, she had really liked the man.

Strictly as a paralegal, of course.

Oh, of course. You didn't even notice how attractive he was.

Sydney ignored her inner voice. The fact that he was an attractive man had nothing to do with her admiration of him. He did excellent work. That's what she cared about. And he wasn't egotistical. He didn't act as if he had something to prove. He was quick and intelligent and he'd showed a lot of common sense.

Yes, and he sure did have a sexy smile.

Sydney smiled in spite of herself. Well, she'd have had to be blind not to notice his smile.

And his eyes. Don't forget his eyes.

Her smile expanded as she exited Memorial Drive and turned right onto Smith Street. Okay. So John Whipple was a very attractive man. So what? That had nothing to do with Sydney's desire to have him come to work for her again.

Liar.

As Sydney entered the parking garage of the building housing her firm, she tried to drive away the thought. But it refused to disappear. *Liar, liar,* it taunted her. *Why don't you admit it? You were attracted to him. That's why you're trying to think up reasons to see him again. That and nothing else!*

Oh, God, she was such a fool, she thought as she parked her car on the sixth level and got out. Hadn't she learned anything from her past experiences? Hadn't she decided long ago that she was no good at romance, no good at sex and absolutely impossible at relationships?

Forget him, Sydney, she lectured herself as she walked into the building and toward the bank of elevators.

Forget him.

John Whipple is not for you.

Chapter Three

"Honestly, John, what's wrong with you this afternoon?" Janet complained.

"I'm sorry. Did you say something?" John looked at his sister, who sat across the dinner table from him. "Guess I wasn't paying attention."

"Say something?" Janet grinned, looking first at their mother, who chuckled and shook her head, then at her husband, who smiled tolerantly. "I asked you a question. Twice."

John shrugged. "Sorry," he repeated. He'd been thinking about Sydney Wells. For about the dozenth time since he'd left her law office Friday afternoon. "What was the question?"

"I asked you if you were planning to take part in the Heights Tennis Tournament this year."

At Janet's mention of the tournament, a dull ache lodged itself in the vicinity of John's heart. He and Andrea had always participated in the Heights Tournament. In fact, Andrea had been one of its most enthusiastic and tireless behind-the-scenes workers. Besides running, tennis had been their favorite sport. He shrugged again, pretending nonchalance. "I don't know. I hadn't thought about it. Why?"

"Well, I bumped into Dave Neff at Randalls the other day, and he asked about you. Said they'd really missed you the last couple of years."

John nodded. He didn't want to discuss the tournament. He didn't want to discuss anything about his private life. Not here. Not now. Maybe not ever again.

He knew how Janet and his mother felt about his withdrawal from most of the activities he and Andrea had participated in together. But they didn't understand. They thought he didn't want to associate himself with those activities because the memories hurt too much.

That might have been the case at first, but it had been almost three years since Andrea's death, and the hurt had become bearable, although John was sure it would never disappear entirely.

No, it was the guilt he felt that had made him change his life-style so drastically. The guilt that kept him away from all of his old activities. Because no matter what the doctors had said, John would never believe that he bore no responsibility for Andrea's collapse and subsequent death. And how could he explain that?

"You know, John," his mother said softly, "it might be good for you to take part in the tournament again."

John looked away. Noticing his son playing with his food, he seized the opportunity to change the subject. "Jeffrey, stop that," he said, hoping his mother and sister would take the hint and drop the subject. "Those peas are to eat, not to play with."

Jeffrey looked up guiltily, but he stopped pushing his peas under his mashed potatoes. His freckled face, so like Andrea's, was a road map of his thoughts and emotions.

John never looked at his son without the reminder of everything he had once had and lost. Everything his children had been deprived of when they'd lost their mother.

"I don't like peas," Jeffrey said, making a face.

"Your father never liked peas, either," Cecelia Appleton said. She ruffled Jeffrey's hair and gave him a fond smile.

"You didn't make him eat his, did you?" Jeffrey asked hopefully.

"Well," Cecelia hedged, her dark eyes twinkling.

Emily piped up. "Daddy says we have to eat our vegetables or we don't get to watch any TV at all." She gave Jeffrey one of her superior ten-year-old-girl looks.

Jeffrey elbowed his sister, and Emily gave John an indignant look. "Daddy!" she said.

"Jeffrey," he warned. "Your sister's right. Now eat your peas."

"I hate you," Jeffrey muttered, giving Emily a murderous look.

"Daddy!" Emily said again.

The children finally settled down, and as John had hoped, the talk turned to other things. But after dinner, when he and Mike, who had insisted on doing the cleanup while the women relaxed in the living room, were rinsing the dishes and putting them in the dishwasher, Mike introduced the subject again.

"I know you don't want to talk about this," he said, "but Janet's worried about you, John."

John stiffened. "There's no reason for her to worry about me."

"She thinks you're alone too much."

"Alone? I'm never alone. How could a man with two kids be alone?"

"You know what I mean."

Yes, John knew what he meant. Sometimes he felt so lonely, he hurt inside, but that kind of loneliness wouldn't be assuaged by the blind dates Janet and Mike had been trying to arrange for the past year.

Like tonight at dinner, they had also been pushing him to participate in neighborhood and church activities. "Look, Mike," he said with a sigh, "I'm not ready. Can we just leave it at that?"

"It's been almost three years," Mike said.

"I'm well aware of how long it's been." As if he could forget. As if he hadn't counted every one of the days, every one of the minutes. It was only in the past year that Andrea's death had begun to be tolerable—that he could think about her without having the memories tear him apart.

"It's not good to isolate yourself," Mike continued relentlessly.

John rammed a plate into the dishwasher harder than he'd meant to. He straightened. "I know you mean well, but drop it, okay? It's my life."

"You can't grieve forever." Mike's blue eyes, kind and sympathetic, met John's. "I know how much you loved Andrea, how close the two of you were. But it's time to let go. Time to find a live woman to share your life with."

John bit back a sharp retort. He nodded. "If I ever meet a woman who interests me, I'll bear that advice in mind."

Yet, as the two of them finished their cleanup, then joined the women and children in the living room, John knew he hadn't been entirely truthful with his brother-in-law. He *had* met a woman who interested him.

Her name was Sydney Scott Wells.

Unfortunately, even if he hadn't lied to her, thereby eliminating any possibility of follow-up on this interest, she wasn't a woman he could ever pursue. He had no interest in involvement with a high-powered career woman like Sydney. What had happened to Andrea had taught him a hard lesson.

He wasn't about to repeat the same mistakes.

Sydney arrived at the office at six-thirty Monday morning, her stomach churning. She hadn't been able to eat this morning, even though she knew it was important to fuel her body in preparation for the challenge ahead. She'd compromised by stuffing a high-fiber bar in her purse with the promise that she'd eat it later.

She'd dressed in her power suit—a lightweight navy wool paired with navy pumps and a cream-colored silk blouse. She wore a discreet gold circle pin on her lapel and matching gold earrings in her ears.

Her team would meet at seven. They were due in Judge Andrews's court at ten. She hoped everyone would be on time today. There was so much to be done.

She wondered how Kara Montgomery was feeling this morning. The McKinseys were bringing Kara to the office about nine, and they would all go over to the court together.

Sydney hoped she'd thought of everything. She had a mental list of things for both Gerri and Norma to take care of today. Norma had promised to come in an hour early.

Norma arrived promptly at seven, flustered and a bit disheveled. Sydney knew the early hour had meant a hardship for her secretary, who was a single mother with two small children, but it couldn't be helped.

At eight, Gerri called. Norma put her through to Sydney.

"Gerri," Sydney said, picking up the phone, "what's wrong? Are you still sick?"

"No, I'm not exactly sick. I, uh, well, I'm pregnant."

Sydney's heart sank. She didn't need this right now.

"And, well, the trouble is, my doctor has confined me to bed, at least for the first three months. I'm sorry, Sydney. I know I should give you notice, but I can't help it. I don't want to take any chances with this pregnancy.''

Sydney closed her eyes. She understood Gerri's position. Gerri had miscarried twice. Of course she wouldn't want to take any chances. Sydney wanted to be glad for Gerri—who really wanted a baby—but right now it was hard to keep from thinking how her paralegal's abrupt departure would affect the office.

Sydney had expected this contingency, sooner or later, but she'd also expected to have months to look for a replacement. When she'd hired Gerri, Gerri had explained that she planned to have children and would probably quit working when she did.

If Gerri hadn't been the best candidate for the job, Sydney would never have hired her. It had been a calculated risk, and now it had backfired.

Gerri was really a top-notch paralegal. It was a shame she had to give up her career. Well, this development just reinforced Sydney's conviction that marriage, children and a career simply didn't mix. Something always got shortchanged. Sydney believed she was wise to understand that. At least she'd never have this kind of problem to worry about.

After she and Gerri hung up, Sydney called Norma into her office. ''Norma, call the Appleton agency and ask them to send that Whipple guy back. Tell them it's an open-ended assignment.''

''All right, Miss Wells.''

''And see if he can get here by nine-thirty.'' Things could have been much worse, she thought. At least now she had a competent paralegal to fall back on. She ignored the pleasurable tingle of anticipation at the thought of having John around for weeks, maybe months, until she could hire another permanent paralegal.

A few minutes later, Norma buzzed Sydney on her intercom. "Miss Wells, the agency says Mr. Whipple isn't available. Is there anyone else you particularly want?"

"What do you mean, he's not available?"

"I, uh... I don't know."

"Didn't you ask them?" Did Sydney have to do *everything?*

"No, I didn't really think—"

"Are they still on the line?" Sydney said, interrupting. She impatiently drummed her fingers against her desk.

"Yes," Norma said meekly.

"Let me talk to them."

"Okay. It's line two. You'll be talking to Mrs. Cameron, the owner of the agency."

Sydney picked up the line. "Mrs. Cameron?"

"Yes?"

"This is Sydney Wells, Mrs. Cameron. Now, listen. I want John Whipple—I guess you call him Joe Whipple—for a long-term assignment. My paralegal is pregnant, and she's not coming back, so I'm really in a bind right now. I need someone good, someone I don't have to train. I'm going to court in just about ninety minutes, so I must have someone I can count on, and John was the best paralegal you've ever sent me. Wherever you've assigned him, change it. Send someone else there, and send him here."

"I'm really sorry, Miss Wells, but I just can't do that."

Sydney frowned. "I don't understand why not. Doesn't Folger & Hubbard's business mean anything to you?" She disliked the implied threat but felt the situation warranted it.

"Of course it does, but John Whipple has, uh, decided not to work temps anymore. He found a full-time job, so even if I wanted to send him to you, I couldn't."

"Found a full-time job? How is that possible? He was just here Friday and he never mentioned it."

"Well, I think it was in the works but he wasn't sure about it until late Friday. How about Patty Howard? You liked her when she worked for you."

"No. I don't want Patty Howard. I want John Whipple," Sydney insisted. "I'll tell you what. You just put me in touch with him. If a permanent position is what he wants, I'll better his other offer, no matter what it is."

"I'm sorry," Janet said. "I can't do that. That would be unethical."

Sydney started to retort, but she realized the woman was right. It *would* be unethical for the agency to undercut one client for another. She had no choice but to agree to their sending Patty Howard, who was an acceptable paralegal but not in John Whipple's class.

Yet, after Sydney hung up, she kept thinking about the conversation. There was something about Janet Cameron's explanation that didn't sit right with Sydney, although she could hardly have called the woman a liar. Why would she lie, anyway? She had nothing to gain and everything to lose.

Still . . . there had been a note of evasiveness in Janet Cameron's voice when she'd said John had another full-time job and contacting him for Sydney would be unethical. Sydney had heard enough falsehoods and evasions of the truth in her interrogation of witnesses to recognize when someone wasn't telling the whole story.

She replayed the conversation in her mind. She could swear there was something fishy about the whole situation, but Sydney was darned if she knew what it was.

John walked Emily and Jeffrey to the bus stop, waited until the school bus came, kissed them goodbye—much to Jeffrey's chagrin—then walked the block and a half back to his house. As always, when the house came into view, he smiled with pleasure.

He loved the house. He and Andrea had bought it the first year they were married. It was a square Victorian with a double-tiered porch set back into the front left-half of the building.

When they'd acquired it, it had been in a sad state of neglect, and they'd had to pour a lot of money, not to mention elbow grease, into it, but all their efforts had been worth it, John thought.

Andrea had been so proud of the house. She'd enjoyed giving dinner parties and inviting their friends over. She'd enjoyed showing off the gleaming hardwood floors and lovingly selected antiques.

The first year after Andrea's death, John had neglected the house. He'd done only what was absolutely necessary in the way of maintenance, but gradually his interest in the place had returned.

Last summer he'd given it a badly needed coat of exterior paint. He'd allowed the children to go with him to choose the color, and they'd picked a lovely shade of slate blue. At first, John had been a little taken aback by the choice—he'd been thinking more in terms of a neutral color—but now he liked the blue, and he thought their mother would have approved of it, too.

The shutters and trim were painted white, and white wicker furniture graced the porches. A huge ash tree shaded one side of the house, and a cluster of redbud trees stood guard on the other side. Several large crape myrtle festooned both sides of the house. Square-clipped boxwood defined the front yard, and borders of seasonal flowers lined the front walk and circled the trees. Soon the fall chrysanthemums would be in full bloom.

The agency's offices took up half of the first floor. The reception and testing area was located in what used to be the front parlor. Their full-time receptionist was on vacation, so Janet was doing double duty right now—filling in for Tammi and acting as the temporary counselor, as well.

The dining room served as Janet's office, where she did all of the interviewing. And the smaller room down the hall, which had been John's study originally, was now his office.

John's primary role in the agency was to develop new business. He also took care of the books, did payroll, taxes, filed government reports and handled the myriad details associated with running a business.

The rest of the downstairs consisted of an old-fashioned kitchen, a pantry, a maid's room, which had been converted into a storeroom for the business, and a bathroom.

Upstairs were John's bedroom, the kids' bedrooms, the fourth bedroom that now served as their living room, an enclosed sun porch across the back of the house where the kids played and did their homework, and another bathroom. They also had the upstairs porch, which they enjoyed all year round.

As John climbed the steps and entered the house, Janet beckoned him into the reception area. "Guess who just called."

"Who?"

Janet made a face. "The Shark."

"Sydney Wells?"

"None other."

John plopped down in front of Janet's desk. "What did she want?"

"You."

John had been afraid of this. "She wanted me back today?"

"Not only for today. A long-term assignment, she said."

"Wonderful," he said dryly. "What did you tell her?"

Janet expelled a noisy sigh. "I think I handled it okay. I said you'd accepted a full-time position with another firm."

"That was quick thinking."

"Yes, but she was furious. She tried not to show it, but she actually threatened to take away her firm's business. She wanted me to put her in touch with you so she could make you a better offer. It seems her paralegal is pregnant and quit, and Miss Wells is up a creek."

"She threatened you?"

"Well, not in so many words, but she implied that her firm was important to us and that we should do whatever it took to keep them happy."

"How'd you get out of that?"

"I told her it would be unethical for us to let her try to hire you away from the other firm."

"More quick thinking."

"Yeah." Janet grinned. "Actually, I was kind of proud of myself for coming up with that on the spur of the moment."

If John really had been a temp and really had taken a full-time job with another of Appleton's clients, it *would* have been unethical for them to steal him away from them, so Janet hadn't exactly lied, John thought thankfully. He still felt uneasy over his lie of omission, though. "So what did she say?"

"What *could* she say? She knew I was right."

"Did you send her someone else?"

"I'm going to call Patty Howard right now."

As John walked off toward his own office, he was filled with regret for his role in deceiving Sydney. He should have known better. My God, one lie only led to others, and if he'd ever doubted that, this morning's events were certainly proof of that axiom.

He hoped this episode would be the end of it. With any luck at all, Patty Howard would be available, she'd go to Folger & Hubbard and Sydney Wells would be satisfied. Because it would be curtains for the agency if Sydney ever found out about his deception.

For the next week, Sydney was so busy she didn't have time to dwell on the puzzle of the Cameron woman's evasiveness. The Montgomery case took all of her energy and time. Although the entire week was taken up with jury selection and routine testimony by expert witnesses, Sydney still felt drained.

It was always this way during a trial. She focused one hundred percent on the proceedings—mentally, physically, emotionally. There was very little left for anything else.

But the following Monday afternoon, Sydney was forced to think about something other than the trial. About four o'clock that afternoon, Patty Howard came into Sydney's office. "Miss Wells, I hate to bother you," she said as Sydney looked up. "I just got a phone call from my mother. My dad's just had another heart attack. I'm going to have to fly up to Minnesota, and I don't know when I'll be back."

Sydney smothered a groan.

"I'm really sorry, Miss Wells," Patty said. "I know this puts you in a bind."

The minute Patty left Sydney's office, she picked up the phone and called the Appleton agency.

"Appleton Legal Temps," said a low, male voice.

"Let me speak to Mrs. Cameron, please," Sydney said.

"I'm sorry, she's out of the office right now. Would you like to leave a message, or can I help you?"

If Sydney hadn't known better, she'd have sworn the voice at the other end of the phone was John Whipple's. *You must be punchy. You've just got John Whipple on the brain.* "This is Sydney Wells, of Folger & Hubbard. To whom am I speaking?"

"This is . . . J. L. Appleton."

Was it her imagination or had there been just the slightest bit of hesitation in his answer? "Mr. Appleton, your firm has provided me with a paralegal for the past week—Patty Howard."

"Yes, I know."

"Did you know that Ms. Howard is going to be unable to complete her assignment?"

"No, I didn't. What's wrong?"

"She's been called out of town on a family emergency. I'm going to need another paralegal—tomorrow. What time is Mrs. Cameron coming back to the office?"

"She should be back in about thirty minutes."

Sydney looked at her watch. It was exactly five o'clock. "How late are you open?"

"Until six."

"Well, would you please tell Mrs. Cameron to call me the minute she returns? I'll be here until at least seven. She can call me directly." Sydney then gave him the number of her private line.

"I'll give her the message. And don't worry, Miss Wells, we'll find you someone good."

After Sydney hung up, she sat looking at the phone for long minutes. Her mind must be playing tricks on her. That couldn't have been John Whipple she'd been talking to. Besides, he'd said his name was J. L. Appleton.

She tried to put the conversation out of her mind. She had testimony to go over, preparations to make for tomorrow in court. But no matter how she tried, she couldn't stop remembering the tone and timbre of J. L. Appleton's voice.

He'd sounded *exactly* like John Whipple!

She tapped her pencil against her desk blotter. Something funny was going on with that agency, and it had to do with John Whipple. How could she find out what it was? First Mrs. Cameron had sounded evasive, and now this. Sydney knew that until she got to the bottom of the mystery, she would not be satisfied.

At five-thirty, Mrs. Cameron had still not returned her call. Sydney made up her mind. She put on her suit jacket, picked up her briefcase and walked out of her office.

Margie, a secretary from the night staff, looked up from the computer terminal at Norma's desk. "Are you leaving, Miss Wells?"

"Yes. And when you finish that brief, leave a copy of it on Norma's desk and put a copy in my office, too. Then you can go back downstairs to the word processing center."

"All right."

"Oh, and if a Mrs. Cameron calls... tell her I've stepped out and I'll call her back."

Margie frowned slightly. "Oh, okay."

"Good night, Margie." Sydney knew the secretary was confused, but she had no intention of explaining her actions.

"Good night, Miss Wells."

Twenty-five minutes later, Sydney pulled up in front of a handsome Victorian house on Heights Boulevard. A discreetly lettered sign that said Appleton Legal Temps hung from the banister of the front porch.

Sydney climbed out of her BMW and locked the door. As she walked up the front walk, she gave her surroundings an appreciative glance. Although she lived in a high-rise condo because she didn't have time to take care of the dozens of responsibilities owning a home entailed, she had always loved big yards with trees and flowers. Some of her happiest memories were of summer afternoons spent lying in the hammock in the backyard of her parents' West University home. That was before they'd had the pool put in, of course. Somehow, her childhood home had never seemed the same to her after that.

Fleetingly, she thought this was an unusual place for an employment agency to be located. Most agencies, particularly those specializing in the legal profession, were located in downtown office buildings, close to the action.

She climbed the porch steps. She could hear several voices, including the high-pitched chatter of children. Someone laughed, then a child giggled. If she hadn't seen the sign proclaiming this to be the temporary agency, she would have thought she was at the wrong address.

She approached the door. It was open, covered only by an outer screened door. There was a doorbell to the left. She pushed the button, and a melodious chime rang out.

A few seconds later, a smiling dark-haired woman appeared behind the screen. She opened the door. "Yes? Can I help you?"

"I'm Sydney Scott Wells. Are you Mrs. Cameron?"

The woman's smile slipped, and for a moment she didn't answer.

Sydney frowned.

"Yes," the woman said, "I'm Janet Cameron. I-I tried to call you about twenty minutes ago, but your secretary said you'd stepped out."

"Yes, well, I had an errand to run near here and thought I might as well stop by and talk to you in person." Something flickered through Janet Cameron's hazel eyes, and Sydney immediately knew her instincts had been right. There was definitely something fishy going on, and Sydney was determined to find out exactly what it was. She smiled pleasantly. "May I come in?"

Janet Cameron hesitated only a second, then she shrugged and sighed. "Yes, of course. I'm sorry. I don't know where my manners are."

Sydney stepped into a bright foyer. The hardwood floors gleamed with polish and loving care. She only had a few seconds to take in the furnishings: a grandfather clock in one corner and an umbrella stand in the

other, and along the wall a small, beautifully refin-
ished walnut bureau and next to it, a Windsor chair.
An oriental carpet runner in shades of soft rose and
blue complemented the rose-blue-and-cream striped
wallpaper and rich walnut moldings, and a soft wa-
tercolor of a rainy Paris street scene hung above the
bureau.

The chatter and laughter had stopped, but Sydney
knew it had come from the big room to the left. Although Janet Cameron started to lead Sydney to the
right, Sydney turned and looked into the other room.

Three pairs of eyes met hers.

Green ones in a little boy who looked to be about
five or six.

Hazel ones in a little girl who looked to be about ten
or eleven.

And warm, dark brown ones that belonged to John
Whipple. A John Whipple who was sitting behind a
big desk and looked as if he belonged there.

Chapter Four

The game was up.

Resigned, John met Sydney's cool gaze. He stood and said, "Hello, Miss Wells."

Behind Sydney, Janet gave John a frantic what-are-we-going-to-do-now? look. He tried to convey with his eyes that there was nothing to be done now but to face the music.

Janet looked as if she wanted to cry as she touched Sydney's arm. "We might as well go in there."

The two women advanced into the room.

"Listen, kids," John said, "you go upstairs and do your homework. I'll be up in a little while."

"But Daddy," Emily protested. "We were just—"

"Emily!"

"Oh, okay." Emily gave John her long-suffering look, but she and Jeffrey left and John heard their footsteps pound up the uncarpeted stairs.

John winced. He wondered what Sydney Wells thought of his unconventional office. If the look on her face was any indication, probably not much.

"Please, Miss Wells," Janet said, "have a seat." She indicated the circular grouping of Queen Anne chairs around a glass-topped mahogany coffee table where applicants sat and filled out their paperwork while waiting to be interviewed.

Sydney walked over to one of the chairs and sat. Her narrow black skirt rode up a few inches, exposing a good-looking knee to go along with her shapely legs. Primly, she tugged it down.

As John sat across from her, the thought flitted through his mind that no matter how she tried to disguise the fact that she was a woman, she would never be entirely successful hiding it. She was simply too attractive, despite her no-frills appearance.

Sydney looked at John, angry glints firing her eyes, making them look even bluer. "Don't you think I deserve some sort of explanation?" she said.

He could see that she was struggling to hold on to her temper. "Yes, of course you do. But first, let's get the names straight, okay? I'm John Appleton." He couldn't help a small smile. "John L. Appleton, to be precise. And you already know my twin sister, Janet Cameron. We're co-owners of the agency."

He didn't try to evade her gaze or the censure he knew she must feel. He knew he was in the wrong here, and if he had to eat crow, he'd do it.

"And just why did you lie to me? Mr. *Appleton?*"

John studied her thoughtfully. "I'm sorry, Miss Wells. I never intended to lie to you."

"Then why did you?"

"If you'll think back, I tried to explain who I was."

"No, you didn't!"

"Yes, I did."

"When?" she said indignantly.

"When you came out of your office that morning and found me talking to your secretary. I started to tell you who I really was, but you cut me off and said you didn't have time to listen to excuses. Remember?"

Her blue eyes narrowed dangerously. "You know I thought you were offering up excuses for being late."

"Yes. And technically, I suppose I was. Because the reason I was late is that Jo Whipple, the temp who was supposed to work for you, had called in sick that morning, and I was the only person available to take her place. And by the time I knew I was going to have to fill in, it was already past the time she'd been due at your firm."

"Then why didn't someone call and tell me so?" she said hotly. "What was I *supposed* to think, when Norma said—"

"Your secretary just assumed I was Jo, and you stormed out of your office before I'd had a chance to correct her."

Janet spoke up, her voice soft but firm. "I tried to call your secretary and tell her about the switch, but I couldn't get through to her, and by the time I could, John was already there. I figured he would explain everything to you."

"I *did* try," John said. Oh, hell. He might as well be completely honest with her. They'd probably blown her business, anyway. "But you ticked me off when you barreled right over me and were rude on top of it. When you as much as told me to shut up, I thought, okay, the hell with her, I won't say another word in explanation. Let her go on thinking whatever she wants to think." He shrugged. "Besides, there was work to be done."

For a long moment, they stared at each other. He wondered what she was thinking. He'd taken a chance saying what he'd said. She might just get up and walk out, taking her firm's lucrative account with her.

He hoped that wouldn't happen, not only because they couldn't afford to lose the business, but because he liked Sydney Wells. He wanted her to respect him.

The grandfather clock in the foyer chimed the quarter hour, and from upstairs, John could hear the children laughing. Beside him, Janet stirred nervously.

Then, to John's surprise and pleasure, Sydney gave him a self-deprecating little smile and said, "I *was* pretty obnoxious, wasn't I?"

John grinned. "Well..."

She nodded. "I guess I owe you an apology, too."

"No, it's okay. We're even."

"I'm going to give you one, anyway," she insisted. "I'm sorry about the way I acted. I was irritated and worried and tired and I took it out on you... and Norma." Her gaze met his unflinchingly.

John decided she had the prettiest blue eyes he'd ever seen. He also decided she was one of the gutsiest women he'd ever met. He liked that about her. He wasn't a man who felt threatened by a strong woman.

"Well..." Sydney stood. "I guess there's no way I'm going to get *you* to come back and work for me, is there?"

John stood, too. "Afraid not, although Janet said you were prepared to better my other offer." He grinned. "And they do say everyone has his price."

Sydney nodded ruefully. "That was pretty arrogant of me, wasn't it?"

"Hey, I was kind of flattered."

She smiled and picked up her briefcase. "Tell me, are you really a paralegal?"

"No, I'm a lawyer."

Her eyes widened. "A lawyer! Really? But you don't practice law?"

John started to reply to the question, then stopped, thought a minute and said, "Do you have any plans for dinner?"

She seemed startled by his question but hesitated only a second before answering. "No."

"Tell you what. Why don't I take you to dinner? I think I owe you at least that much after what's happened."

"You don't owe me anything, Mr. Apple—"

"And please call me John."

Those bright blue eyes studied him for a moment, then she smiled warmly.

She should smile more often, John thought.

"I'd love to go to dinner with you, John."

"Good," John said, pleased, although he wasn't sure what he was going to do about the kids. Maybe Janet would take them home with her.

"And I'd like for you to call me Sydney," she continued. She stuck out her hand. "Is it a deal?"

As John took her smaller hand in his, shaking it solemnly, he wondered if he had lost his sanity. He had promised himself he would stay far away from Sydney Wells, and here he was, doing just the opposite.

Oh, hell, no big deal. He would take her to dinner—after all, he did owe her—and then, tomorrow, he would put her out of his mind.

Sydney waited downstairs while John and his sister went upstairs to what Sydney assumed were John's living quarters. Although John had said he would call a teenager who lived down the street to come and stay with his children, Janet had said her husband was at a meeting and wouldn't be home until late, so she would stay with the kids while Sydney and John went to dinner.

Before Janet went upstairs, she'd offered her hand to Sydney, and apologized once more. Her apology was polite enough and seemed sincere enough, but Sydney sensed a reserve in the woman. She had the uncomfortable feeling that Janet didn't like her very much.

Although Sydney should have been used to that reaction—Lord knows, she got it often enough—for some reason, Janet Cameron's lack of friendliness bothered her. After all, Sydney had done nothing to Janet. It was really the other way around.

Then Sydney realized that Janet might simply be reacting to John's unexpected dinner invitation. Perhaps Janet didn't like the idea that John had asked her out. But why she should disapprove, Sydney couldn't imagine. It wasn't like this was a date, or anything.

Sydney was still thinking about Janet when John came downstairs a few minutes later, looking handsome and casual in dark pants and a tan corduroy sports coat. Sydney eyed him appreciatively and thought about how long it had been since she'd gone to dinner with a good-looking man. It had to have been at least six months.

Cliff O'Malley, from the prosecutor's office, had been her last attempt to date—and that episode had been as unsatisfying as most of the others she'd experienced over the past few years. As long as she and Cliff were talking shop, they'd been fine, but the minute the talk turned to anything else, Sydney had felt tongue-tied and inadequate. And she knew Cliff had been bored. He certainly hadn't called her again.

Of course, tonight wasn't like that, Sydney reminded herself again. Tonight wasn't a date, it was business.

"Do you like Mexican food?" John asked, taking her arm and purposefully steering her out the front door.

"I'm passionate about Mexican food."

He grinned. "Good. Me, too." They walked out onto the porch.

The setting sun had gilded the world a rosy orange, and Sydney thought about how twilight could either be the loveliest or loneliest time of day.

"Do you mind walking a few blocks?" John said when they reached the sidewalk.

"No, not at all." It was a bit cool, but not unpleasantly so—perfect for walking, Sydney thought.

"We'll walk, then. I'm taking you to a neighborhood restaurant owned by some friends of mine. They serve the best Mexican food you ever ate."

"Good. I'm starved." Sydney had forgotten to eat lunch today, which was par for the course with her. And all she'd had for breakfast was half a grapefruit and dry toast because she'd forgotten to buy margarine.

They didn't talk much on the short walk, but Sydney didn't feel awkward about the silence. Somehow, with John, she felt relaxed and perfectly natural. Less than ten minutes after starting out, they arrived at a small restaurant with a sign proclaiming it to be Maria's Mexican Café.

"Maria and Hector Alvarez are two of the nicest people you'll ever meet," John said, opening the front door for Sydney. Warm food smells greeted her as she walked in ahead of John.

They had no sooner been seated by a smiling, dark-eyed waitress dressed in a colorful Mexican dress when a small dark man with a beaming smile approached their table.

"John!" he exclaimed. "It's so good to see you."

"Hello, Hector."

"And with such a beautiful young lady!" Hector turned his brilliant smile on Sydney.

"I'd like you to meet my friend, Sydney Scott Wells," John said. "Sydney, this is Hector Alvarez."

"Hello, Mr. Alvarez," Sydney said, smiling.

"Oh, yes, so very beautiful," Hector said. He reached for her hand, bowing over it and, to Sydney's amusement, kissing it. He sighed elaborately. "John, where did you find her?"

John chuckled. "You wouldn't believe me if I told you." He looked around. "Where's Maria tonight?"

Hector rolled his eyes. "At her mother's house. You know how it is with Maria. When Mama calls . . ."

John and his friend talked for a few more minutes, and Sydney thought how nice it was to see two men so relaxed with each other, so obviously not in competition with each other. It seemed to her that most of the men she knew were in a constant state of one-upmanship.

They bragged about their conquests, both at work and in the romance department, and showed off their possessions with an air of I'll-bet-you-can't-beat-that. Sydney hated men like that. Men like that were always put off by her, too. They seemed to require the type of woman who would hang on their every word and say little more than, "You're so wonderful, honey."

Soon, Hector left, and within minutes, John and Sydney each had a frosty margarita in front of them and were sharing a huge basket of hot, crispy tostados and a bowl of the best picante sauce Sydney had ever tasted.

"These are wonderful," Sydney said, eating enthusiastically.

"I like a woman with a good appetite," John commented after a few minutes.

Sydney could feel her face heating. What was wrong with her? She'd been stuffing her face. That was sure a great way to impress a man. "I didn't have any lunch."

"Don't apologize!" He grinned. "I meant it. I can't stand women who pick at their food."

"No one's ever accused me of that." To get the subject off her, Sydney said, "Tell me how a lawyer ends up in the temporary employment business."

His smile faded and he shrugged. "When my wife died suddenly three years ago, everything changed for me. I completely reevaluated my life and found that things that had once been important to me no longer were. Besides, I needed to find a way to be around for my kids."

"I'm sorry about your wife."

He nodded. "Thanks." He took a sip of his drink, then set the glass down. "I still miss her."

Sydney swallowed. It was obvious that he had loved his wife very much. She could see it in his eyes and hear it in his voice. What must it be like to have someone love you like that? Miss you like that? A funny kind of emptiness slid into her stomach.

"To go back to your question," John said, "Janet had worked as a counselor for a temporary employment agency, and she got the idea of an agency specializing in legal temps. We decided to go into business together, and I converted the bottom floor of my house into our offices."

He had shaken off his momentary sadness, Sydney could see, and she struggled to shake off her own nameless yearning. "And it's worked out well?"

"Yeah, we've done okay. We'd like more business, of course, but we're holding our own."

"Do you like the work?"

He hesitated. "Most of the time."

"Who did you work for when you practiced law?"

"I was a partner at Chasan & Jeglinski."

Sydney was impressed. Chasan & Jeglinski was one of the top five law firms in Houston, only slightly smaller than Folger & Hubbard. "Good firm," she said.

John nodded. "Yes. Andrea—my wife—was a partner there, too. In fact, that's how we met, when we both went to work for them straight out of law school."

Just then, their waiter came up to take their order. Once he was gone, John said, "Tell me about you."

Sydney shrugged. "There's not much to tell. You know most of it already. I've been a partner at the firm for five years, and my specialty, actually my passion, is children's rights. I occasionally take on other kinds of cases, but not often."

He smiled. "No kids of your own?"

Normally, Sydney felt uncomfortable talking about her private life, but his dark eyes were so warm and he seemed really interested, and she suddenly found herself saying things she'd never intended to say. "No, I'm single and a big disappointment to my mother."

"How can you be a big disappointment to your mother? You're successful and the work you do is worthwhile, admirable even."

Sydney felt a warm glow at his praise. "Well, that's how I feel, but my mother's idea of success is marriage and children."

He nodded. "And it's not yours."

"No."

"Do you want to get married someday?"

It was on the tip of Sydney's tongue to say no. Instead, she shrugged. "I don't know. I suppose if I met someone I wanted to marry..." *What on earth made me say that?* She took another swallow of her margarita. "Actually, I don't think marriage and being the kind of lawyer I am mix very well."

John nodded thoughtfully. "It takes time and work to make marriage successful."

"And I barely have enough time now." For some perverse reason, she wished he'd disagree with her.

"You're wise to know yourself so well." He smiled. "Of course, your mother may never accept that. Mothers want grandchildren."

"My mother already has six grandchildren with another on the way. She doesn't need any from me." Sydney hated feeling the bitterness that talking about her mother's expectations always produced.

"So you've got siblings..."

"Yes. I'm the youngest of four girls. My sisters are very traditional, not like me at all. Sometimes I wonder if..."

"Wonder if what?" John prompted.

"I don't know. My father always wanted a boy, and when I was born, he finally realized he wasn't going to get one, so he named me after himself and raised me like the son he never had." Sydney drew circles in the condensation on her glass. "And I, well, I've always wondered if I would have turned out the same way if I'd been treated like my sisters, or if the way I am is my natural state."

"And how are you?" John said quietly.

"Driven. A workaholic. Not . . . feminine."

"What!" He made a sound of disbelief. "That's ridiculous. Driven, yes. A workaholic, probably. But *unfeminine?* No way."

Something hot and sweet twisted through Sydney at the warm glow in John's eyes, the unmistakable gleam of admiration and sincerity she saw and felt. She knew her cheeks had flushed and was grateful for the subdued lighting in the restaurant.

What was it about John Appleton that had caused her to tell him things she never admitted to anyone? She hoped John didn't think she'd been fishing for a compliment, because that had been the farthest thing from her mind when she'd said what she'd said. In fact, she couldn't imagine what had even possessed her to admit that she felt unfeminine. Had always felt unfeminine.

"Why on earth would you think you're not feminine?" John said.

Sydney waited until their waiter, who had approached with their plates, served them. She chose her words carefully. "I'm too tall, for one thing."

"I happen to like tall women."

Sydney shrugged. "Most men seem to be intimidated by tall women."

"You don't hang around with the right men." John took a forkful of his Chilé Relleno and ate it. "Okay, so you're tall. What else?"

Sydney ate some of her enchiladas before answering. "I don't know how to talk to men."

John laughed out loud. "Seems to me you're doing just fine."

"I feel comfortable with you," Sydney blurted out, then wished she could take the words back. What if he thought she was flirting with him? *Well, would that be so bad?*

"Good." His eyes were warm as they met her gaze. "I feel comfortable with you, too."

Shyness attacked Sydney, and she had to look away. She ate some rice and beans, then more of her enchilada. When she looked up again, John's eyes twinkled with amusement. "Stop laughing at me."

"I'm not laughing at you," he said softly. "I'm just wondering how someone as obviously intelligent as you are can possibly think of yourself as unfeminine. Don't you ever look in the mirror?"

Sydney blushed. Once again, she was thankful for the dim lighting. "I look in the mirror all the time. That's the problem." Besides, she didn't need to look in the mirror. Men's reactions to her told a much more accurate story.

"You must be blind, then, because you're a beautiful woman."

"Could we please talk about something else?" Sydney said, completely embarrassed by the turn the conversation had taken. It was sweet of John to try to make her feel good about herself, but enough was enough. She wasn't beautiful, not by a long shot, and she knew it. She was too tall, her feet were too big, her hair was too straight and she had no feminine wiles whatsoever.

"Okay," John said agreeably. "If that'll make you less uncomfortable. What do you want to talk about?" He ate some more of his food.

"You. What kind of law did you practice?"

"I was a tax law specialist."

"Tax law!" Somehow, John didn't fit the role.

He grinned. "Sounds boring, doesn't it?"

"Actually, yes."

"It wasn't. I really enjoyed it. I was good at it, too. What kind of law did you think I practiced?"

"You look like a criminal lawyer."

"That was Andrea's speciality." At the mention of his wife, the grin disappeared.

Sydney hesitated a moment, then said, "Your wife must have been very young when she died."

"Thirty-six."

Only two years older than Sydney was now. "What happened?" she asked softly.

He sighed and laid down his fork. He took a final swallow of his margarita, then set the empty glass down. "We always jogged together. Every morning. I ran ten miles a day, but Andrea could never run more than six miles at a time, no matter how hard she tried. I always teased her about it, because she was so competitive, and she hated me to best her at anything."

Sydney watched his face as he talked. Although his voice was impassive, his eyes mirrored his emotions.

"On that particular morning, I said something like, 'Why don't you admit it? There are some things a man can do better than a woman, like run.' She said she'd never admit that, that she'd run as far as me that morning if it killed her."

Sydney's heart seemed to stop. She knew what was coming and she wanted to tell him it was okay, he didn't have to say the words out loud.

"I egged her on. That's what I can't forget. I egged her on, and fifteen minutes later, about mile eight and a half, she collapsed," he said tonelessly. "She was dead before the ambulance arrived."

"Oh, God," Sydney said. "How awful for you."

"The doctors said it was an aneurism. That it didn't matter that she was pushing herself. That it could have happened even if she'd been sitting quietly." He laughed, the sound ragged. "I know they were telling me the truth, but that doesn't help. I still feel guilty. I still feel responsible."

"Oh, John, surely you don't blame yourself!"

"Who else is there?" he said bitterly. "I'm alive, and Andrea's dead. And how can the doctors be so sure the jogging had nothing to do with what happened?"

"John, even I, who know very little about medicine, know that an aneurism doesn't just happen. If a person has one, it can remain stationary for years, causing no harm, and then one day... boom. It's all over."

"Look, I know you mean well, Sydney, and I appreciate it, but let's change the subject, okay? I really don't want to talk about this. I usually don't. I don't know why I did tonight.''

Sydney impulsively reached across the table and touched his hand. "I'm glad you trusted me enough to tell me."

He turned his hand palm up and closed it around hers. Their gazes met and held for several heartbeats. Sydney didn't even realize she was holding her breath until he released her hand after first giving it a little squeeze.

It was only then that she admitted to herself how very much she wanted John Appleton to keep trusting her.

And how very much she wanted to keep seeing him.

Chapter Five

John wasn't sure what was wrong with him, but no matter how he tried, he couldn't get Sydney out of his mind. All week long, whatever he was doing, his thoughts kept straying to Monday night.

He kept picturing her as she'd looked sitting across the table from him. Her hair swinging softly around her face, shining honey gold in the candlelight. Her eyes, dark blue and intense, as they watched him. Her slender fingers wrapped around the stem of her glass. The vulnerable sweep of her jaw. Her soft mouth— just a little too wide, but appealing, nevertheless.

Where had she ever gotten the idea she wasn't feminine? From her mother?

John had known Sydney was trying to hide her femininity, but he'd thought the reason had something to do with her profession. He'd figured Sydney thought she had to look tough to succeed. But she really *believed* she wasn't attractive.

The woman was beautiful, in his opinion. True, she might not be everyone's type. She certainly wasn't fragile and clinging, and she didn't bat her eyes and act helpless, like some women. But John had never been attracted to women like that, anyway.

No, he liked women who were smart and strong, witty and confident. A match for him. A challenge for him.

Sydney was all of that . . . and more.

But Monday night had only reinforced John's decision that, just as he'd suspected, it would be foolhardy to entertain any idea of an involvement with Sydney. The two of them were on completely different courses in life.

Sydney had as much as admitted she wasn't interested in marriage and children. Sure, she'd *said* if the right man came along she might be, but she hadn't fooled John. She was obviously consumed by her career, just as driven and competitive as he had once been. And that was not the kind of life John intended to ever lead again—no matter how much he might miss the stimulation of his law practice. His kids deserved more than that. And he would give them more than that.

It was a shame, though, he reflected with regret. He had enjoyed himself Monday night. He had forgotten how satisfying good conversation and good food and the company of an attractive woman could be.

Sydney had reminded him of all that, of how much he was missing, of how much he had lost.

It was actually kind of funny. All of Janet's and Mike's and his mother's reminders and lectures hadn't been able to do what one evening in Sydney's company had accomplished.

John smiled, remembering how Janet had acted when he had arrived home after saying good-night to Sydney and seeing her off in her car.

"Well?" she'd said with undisguised curiosity as he entered the house. "How was it?"

"Nice."

"Nice?" She looked skeptical.

"Yes, nice. I enjoyed myself. She's an interesting woman."

Janet made a face. "Oh, she's interesting, all right."

John didn't like her tone of voice. "Why do you say it that way?"

Janet shrugged. "I don't know." Her hazel eyes met his. "Yes, I do know. I don't like that woman, John."

"You don't even know her."

"I know that she acts as if she's better than other people."

He frowned. "No, she doesn't."

"Why are you defending her?"

"Because you're not being fair to her. You've seen her exactly once, and you've already formed an opinion. That isn't like you, Jan."

Janet's eyes widened. "Why, you're *attracted* to her, aren't you? I can't believe it."

John rarely got angry with Janet. Being twins, the two of them were generally on the same wavelength, plus Janet was a noncombative person with a sunny disposition. Yet now he could almost feel his blood pressure going up.

"Just what is it you can't believe, Jan? Is it so hard to believe that I might be interested in a woman? Hell, you're the one who's been so hot to get me to start dating again."

"Yes, but, my God, John, not with someone like Sydney Wells."

"There's not a thing wrong with Sydney Wells. She's attractive, intelligent and good company. And you're right. I *am* attracted to her, and not just a little bit, either."

Janet looked stunned.

John's anger evaporated as quickly as it had formed. "Let's not fight, okay? I'm sorry. I shouldn't have snapped at you."

"I . . . it's okay. It's none of my business who you date. I know that."

"Aw, Janet, I know you worry about me." He pulled her close for a quick hug. "But you don't need to. And you don't need to worry about Sydney, either, because even though she *does* interest me, I won't be seeing her again."

Sydney knew she needed all her wits about her during this trial, but the day after her dinner with John, she found her mind wandering, and she had to force herself to stop thinking about him and about their evening together.

All day Tuesday, she couldn't wait to get back to the office to see if he'd called her. Anticipation rippled through her as she accepted her message slips from Norma. But when she hurriedly sorted through them, there was no message from John.

Among the messages was one from her father. She knew he wanted an update on her day in court. Thrusting thoughts of John from her mind, she picked up the phone.

"Hi, Dad," she said when he answered.

"Hi. How'd things go today?"

"Good. Real good, I think."

"Who testified today?"

"The defense experts."

"The Bartlett woman?"

Her father was referring to one of the state social workers—a woman that had worried Sydney because from everything Sydney had been able to see, the woman sounded very credible—and she was going to testify that, in her opinion, Kara would be better off with her mother. "Ada Bartlett will testify tomorrow."

"You worried?"

Sydney shrugged. "Not really. I think I can punch a few holes in her testimony."

"I know you can!"

They talked a few more minutes, then her father said, "It's really going to be fun when this trial is over. I have a feeling the offers are going to come pouring in."

"Dad—"

"I'm so proud of you, Sydney."

After they hung up, Sydney sighed. She wondered what would happen if she didn't win the case. Her father would be awfully disappointed. She would be, too, but not for the same reasons.

Still thinking about her father, she forgot about John for a while, but that night she thought about him again. She decided he had probably not called her today because he thought it was too soon. Yes, that was it. He would call her tomorrow.

But on Wednesday there was no message from him.

And on Thursday, when she returned to her office from court, and again there was no message, she asked Norma twice if there were any others that she might have forgotten to give her.

Norma gave her a funny look. "No, Miss Wells, that's it. Were you expecting one in particular?"

"No, no. Not really."

Sydney told herself she didn't care that he hadn't called, but a funny little ache tightened her chest.

John, I thought you liked me!

Why didn't he call? Surely she hadn't imagined the interest sparking his eyes. When he'd told her she was beautiful, she was positive he'd meant it. And when he'd taken her hand, she could have sworn he'd felt the same awareness she'd felt.

So, if that were true, why didn't he call? God, what was wrong with her that she couldn't even get to first base, let alone home plate, with a man who interested her?

Why don't you call him?

Sydney swiveled her chair around to look out her twenty-third-story window. Now that the clocks had been turned back, and Houston was once more on standard time, dusk fell early. It wasn't even six o'clock and already the sky had purpled in the east.

Why didn't she call him?

After all, she was a woman of the nineties. Didn't women of the nineties go after what they wanted? They sure as heck didn't sit around waiting for things to happen. They made things happen. *She* had always made things happen.

So call him.

Sydney chewed on the end of her pencil, a habit she'd been trying to break for months, with no success. She watched as low-hanging clouds scuttled across the sky. It was supposed to rain tomorrow, she remembered.

Should she call him?

Why not? If you'd been to someone's home for dinner, you'd call and reciprocate or at least call and thank them, so why should the rules be any different because he'd taken her to a restaurant?

That was it. She'd call and ask *him* to dinner.

But what would he think if she did? Would he think she was going after him?

So what if he does?

Yes. So what if he did? Wasn't the direct approach better than playing those silly games men and women played? Besides, Sydney was no good at those games. Never had been.

She swiveled her chair around again, looked at the phone for a few seconds, then took a deep breath and picked up the receiver.

* * *

John was halfway up the stairs when the phone rang. For a second, he debated whether to take the rest of the stairs two at a time and grab the call upstairs or race down and get it in the office.

Down won.

"Appleton Legal Temps," he said, snatching it up before the recorder could kick in.

"I was beginning to think no one was going to answer."

He recognized Sydney's voice immediately. Pleasure he couldn't deny filled his voice as he said, "You caught me on the stairs. It took me a while to decide whether to race up or race down."

"You mean your business phone rings upstairs, too?"

"Well, yes," he admitted. "Although I turn the sound down in the evenings and mostly just let the recorder pick up any calls that come in."

"And I thought I was a workaholic."

"It's not as bad as it sounds. Hardly anyone ever calls after hours." After a slight pause during which she didn't say anything, he added, "So how's your week been? The new temp working out all right?"

"Yes, she's working out fine."

"How about the trial?"

"The trial's moving along, and I feel pretty good about it, except that Kara's mother testified today, and she was a darned good witness. Much better than I would have guessed."

"Is that going to be a problem?"

He could almost hear her shrug. "I don't know. It's impossible to read this jury. Sometimes I think Kara's case is a shoo-in. Other times I'm not so sure. Her mother made a very sympathetic witness. Even I felt sorry for her."

"How much longer do you expect the trial to go?"

"Another couple of days, I think. Final arguments should come about Wednesday."

John would love to hear Sydney give her final argument on this case.

There was another awkward little pause. Then she said, "Listen, John, the reason I called was to thank you for dinner Monday and to offer a payback."

"A payback?"

She laughed, and to John's ears the laugh sounded a bit forced, a bit false. "You know, reciprocity. I'd like to take *you* to dinner."

"That's not necessary."

"I know it's not necessary. I want to. Are you by any chance free tomorrow night?"

"Uh, tomorrow night? Tomorrow night is Friday." He had something going on tomorrow night, he was sure of it. "Wait a minute." He flipped the calendar page over. There it was. "I'm sorry, Sydney. I knew there was something. Tomorrow night there's a musical at the kids' school, and I promised to take them."

"Oh, well, in that case..."

He could tell she didn't believe him. Her voice had that hollow sound to it. Damn! Why had she called? Why had she put him in this position? He'd probably hurt her feelings. He *knew* he'd hurt her feelings.

"Could we make it Saturday night, instead?" he heard himself say.

"I hate to make you give up your Saturday night. I just thought—"

"I *want* to," he interjected. He did want to. That was the problem.

After they'd settled on a time and a place, and John got directions to her condo, they hung up. As John slowly climbed the stairs, he had a feeling he might be sorry for his impulsive action a few minutes ago. It would have been much better to just let Sydney's feelings be hurt. She would have gotten over it. A turndown of an invitation wasn't that big a deal. This way, seeing her again, was likely to cause much bigger problems.

For both of them.

Sydney worked on polishing her final argument until three o'clock on Saturday. Then, to the obvious surprise of Norma, who had agreed to come in for the day, she packed up her briefcase and breezed out of the office.

"I'm going home, Norma. You can go, too."

Riding down in the elevator, Sydney chuckled as she thought about the expression on Norma's face.

Sydney pulled into the underground garage of her high-rise building at three-thirty. She waved at Pete, the daytime garage attendant. After a minute, he waved back, but she saw the expression of surprise on his face. She grimaced. Was she normally so preoccupied that a simple wave was enough to cause raised eyebrows?

Ten minutes later, she was unlocking the door to her eighteenth-floor condominium. Her Post Oak area building was twenty stories high, and each story had six condos. The four larger ones were corner units, the two smaller ones were inside units. Sydney had an inside unit, but it faced southeast, so she had a magnificent view of downtown Houston, which she loved, and a completely private patio, which she also loved.

She looked around the condo with a critical eye. Her once-a-week maid had been in yesterday, so the place was clean. She wondered what John would think of it and tried to see it through his eyes.

The condo consisted of a large combination living/dining area, a small kitchen, a guest bath, two bedrooms—one small and one large—the master bath, and a tiny utility room just big enough for a stack washer and dryer, and a sink.

Lifeless, she thought, studying the impeccably decorated, but completely impersonal living area. When the decorator had suggested the black-and-white color scheme, with touches of red and yellow to give it "oomph," as she'd called it, Sydney had agreed without much interest or enthusiasm.

"As long as it looks good, I don't care what you do," she'd said, giving the decorator carte blanche. Actually, if she'd thought no one else would ever see it, she wouldn't have even cared if it looked good. She'd only bought the condo to give herself a tax break and to have a secure, safe place to live—somewhere she wouldn't be frightened to come home to when she worked late.

Now, though, she saw what John would see. A place where there were no personal touches. A place where Sydney didn't spend enough time to make it into a real home. A place without life.

A lonely place.

Sydney shook off the depressing thought and walked to her bedroom. She tossed her briefcase on the bed, shrugged out of her suit coat and walked to the closet. She slid open the mirrored door, flipped on the interior light and walked inside. After hanging up her suit coat and divesting herself of the rest of her work clothes, she stood in her underwear and surveyed the contents of her closet.

Dozens of suits in subdued neutral colors lined the long wall. They were color-coded and arranged according to seasons. Both the skirts and jackets hung on the top tier of a divided rack. On the bottom rack, at least a hundred blouses hung, also color-coded.

On the right wall of the closet were Sydney's casual clothes, and to the left her dressy clothes. Her shoes were neatly boxed and labeled and stacked in rows on shelves.

She needed something dressy for tonight. The selection of dressy clothes was pitiful, she decided, thinking that was another sad commentary on her life, just as the parking attendant's reaction had been.

She sighed. What should she wear tonight? She had made reservations at Brennan's, one of her favorite restaurants. People usually dressed up to go to Brennan's.

She eyed her small selection of dresses, finally settling on a black, long-sleeved, jewel-necked silk crepe with a self-belt. It was awfully plain, but it would have to do. It was the best she had, other than a cocktail suit with sequins, which she'd never liked and which was much too fussy, anyway.

By six-thirty, she'd had her bath and washed her hair. She'd tried curling it, with no success, and finally resigned herself to wearing it in the same simple style she affected for work. She'd experimented with eye shadows, but thought they all looked ridiculous on her, so ended up with the touch of blue-gray she always wore. She'd put on one of those new wine-colored lipsticks, but thought it made her look like a vampire, so she'd wiped it off and gone back to her same old rosy pink.

When it came to jewelry, she really wished she had something glitzy. Some big earrings with rhinestones or something. But she didn't. Her entire jewelry collection consisted of six or seven pairs of sedate gold earrings, a thick gold chain necklace, a thin gold chain necklace, a gold circle pin, an onyx and gold bracelet and matching earrings, and small pearl earrings with a matching two-strand necklace.

She sighed.

She wore the pearls. A small black suede evening purse and two-inch black suede pumps completed her outfit.

Promptly at seven, Bruce, the lobby security guard, announced John's arrival. "Send him up," she said. She pressed her stomach to still the sudden flutter of nerves.

The doorbell chimed.

When Sydney opened the door, her breath caught. She had forgotten how attractive John was, how... sexy. And John in a dark, pin-striped suit was even better-looking and sexier than John in anything else she'd seen him in so far.

He smiled. "Hi." His gaze swept over her. "Don't you look nice."

The approval in his warm, dark eyes made her insides feel like someone had poured hot liquid through her.

"Thanks. You don't look so bad yourself. Come on in."

He walked past her into the condo and headed straight for the expanse of picture-window and patio doors. Sydney had opened the floor-length white drapes, and nighttime Houston, with its glittering expanse of lights, beckoned.

"Wow," he said. "What a view."

Sydney walked up beside him. He smelled wonderful, she thought, from some kind of tangy-scented, male cologne. "It is spectacular, isn't it? Would you like to go outside for a while?"

He looked at his watch. "Didn't you say our reservations were for seven forty-five?"

"Yes."

"Perhaps we'd better get going, then. Maybe when we come back?"

Maybe when we come back.

The words sent a thrill through Sydney, conjuring up all sorts of exciting images. She smiled. "All right."

When they got to the parking garage, John apologized for his Bronco. "Trucks aren't exactly made for high heels."

"I'm fine," Sydney assured him as he helped her up. The feel of his strong hands on her waist made her tingle inside.

She couldn't help silently laughing at herself on the way to the restaurant. She had never been the kind of woman who needed or wanted a man's help. Yet tonight, there was something very appealing about playing the subordinate role. She actually wanted doors held open for her, an arm at her elbow, someone else taking the lead.

Later, seated across from John at a table overlooking the courtyard, she wondered what it was about him that produced such contradictory emotions in her. She felt more relaxed and comfortable around him than she'd felt with anyone in a long time, yet overriding this feeling was a delicious tension and awareness of him as a man.

She knew what produced the last feeling. She was attracted to him sexually.

It was the comfort she tried to analyze. Perhaps this feeling came from the fact that he wasn't one of those men who wanted to talk of nothing but themselves. He actually paid attention to her. Listened to her. As if he really cared what she said.

Yes, that was it.

John seemed truly interested in her, and he let her know it.

She smiled. He made her feel special. He certainly didn't make her feel as if he thought she was boring and one-dimensional, as a long-ago boyfriend had said when they'd broken up. Sydney grimaced inwardly. That night had been one of the low points of her life. It had been the only time she'd really thought she was in love, and when Ken made his dismissive assessment of her character, she felt more inferior and inadequate than at any time before or since. Even now, remembering, the old hurt rose to claim her, and she had to fight it back.

"So how's your final argument coming along?" John asked as they waited for their first course of turtle soup.

"It's ready, I think. I did final polishing today. Of course, there may be some minor changes after the last couple of witnesses testify... you know, if something is said that I think needs to be refuted. That kind of thing."

"Yes, I remember." He smiled, but Sydney thought there was a look of longing in his eyes, which he quickly masked.

"Do you miss it?" she asked softly. "Do you miss practicing law?"

He hesitated for a moment, then nodded. "Yes, I have to admit it. Sometimes I do miss it." He picked up a roll and split it open.

"Tell me something," Sydney said, breaking off a piece of her own roll. "I know you said you stopped practicing law because you wanted to be around for your kids, but couldn't you have just scaled down your workload and accomplished the same thing?"

He gave her a rueful look. "I suppose I could have. At the time, though, I was so torn up emotionally, I wasn't really thinking straight. And now, well, now it's too late.''

Sydney frowned. ''Why is it too late?'' She ate a piece of roll.

Their waiter arrived with their soup, and John waited until the man had served them before replying. ''Well, there are two reasons. First and most important is the kids. I promised myself I'd be there for them. Second, there's the agency. I couldn't walk out on Janet. And even if I could, I know myself, and I know how easy it would be to get caught up in all that again.''

''All what again?'' Sydney tasted her soup. As usual, it was perfection.

''You know. The excitement. The challenge. The kill.''

Sydney smiled quizzically. ''The kill? I thought you were a tax lawyer.''

John smiled. ''Well, I was kind of a big-time tax lawyer.''

''He said modestly,'' she added, chuckling at his sheepish look.

''I'm tired of talking about me,'' he said. ''Let's talk about you for a while.''

''Why don't you tell me about your children first? How old are they?''

''Emily's ten and Jeffrey's six.'' His voice rang with pride. ''They're great kids, although Emily worries me sometimes.''

''Why?''

''She's a perfectionist. Extremely competitive. Exactly like her mother was.''

"What's wrong with that?" Sydney was a perfectionist and competitive, herself.

"I don't want Emily to be that driven. It certainly had disastrous consequences for Andrea."

"Oh, John, surely you realize that what happened to your wife would have happened to her even if she'd been June Cleaver, at home baking cookies all day. I don't think aneurisms choose their victims according to personality types."

"We don't really know that. Maybe if Andrea had taken life a little easier, relaxed more, she would have lived longer." By now their salads had arrived, and he picked up his fork and speared a crouton. "I just don't want Emily to always think she has to be number one. It's not healthy to push yourself that way."

"I don't think I agree with you," Sydney said. "What's wrong with trying to do your best?"

John didn't answer for a while, and Sydney grew a bit uncomfortable under his steady gaze. She ate some of her salad and wondered if she should have kept her opinion to herself. After all, he was Emily's father. What did Sydney know about kids, anyway? Being a children's advocate wasn't the same as being a parent and living with a child twenty-four hours a day.

"You're right that there's nothing wrong with trying to do your best," John finally said. "But I don't want my children to be one-dimensional. I want them to have full and happy lives. Lives that include marriage and children and fulfilling work and lots of time to play and have fun."

Sydney felt as if he'd punched her in the stomach. *One-dimensional.* Was that what he thought of her?

Had she been kidding herself when she told herself that John really liked her? That he was interested in her?

You're the most boring, one-dimensional person I've ever known.

Ken's old taunt reverberated in her mind. The disgusted, pitying look he'd given her was as freshly wounding as if it had just happened.

It *did* just happen, Sydney thought.

The only reason John had agreed to tonight's dinner is that I'm a valuable client for his agency.

For the rest of their meal, the thought hammered at Sydney. No matter how she tried, it refused to go away. Everything John said after that, she analyzed and looked for the hidden meanings.

He hadn't wanted to go out with her again. He'd agreed to dinner because when she called and asked him out, he hadn't wanted to jeopardize her business.

He had no personal feelings for her. She had been deluding herself, thinking he felt the way she felt because that's what she wanted to think.

You're so stupid! Sure, he has personal feelings for you. He feels sorry for you! He thinks you're one-dimensional.

By the time they'd finished dinner, Sydney was miserable. She knew John felt the change in atmosphere between them, because his conversation had become strained, and he kept looking at her as if he was trying to figure out what was going on in her mind.

Sydney couldn't wait to get home.

She couldn't wait to get away from him. Away from those eyes.

She almost laughed, thinking how excited she'd been about this evening earlier.

Dinner was finally over. And when the waiter brought the bill, Sydney snatched it up before John could even think about paying it.

"I'm the host tonight," she said stiffly, avoiding John's eyes.

As they walked out into the navy night and waited for John's Bronco to be brought around, Sydney wanted to cry. She never cried. The last time she'd cried, she'd been ten years old and gotten her arm broken when her horse threw her. She still remembered what her father had said.

"Only weak people cry, Sydney."

She forced the tears away.

Chapter Six

What the devil was wrong with her?

John searched his mind for clues on the silent ride home. He couldn't imagine what had brought about her change in behavior, but it was cold enough in this car to freeze Miami in August. To relieve the tension and silence, he inserted a Lyle Lovett CD.

"Do you like Lyle Lovett?" he asked as music flooded the car.

She shrugged. "I'd never even heard of him until he married Julia Roberts."

That statement was a perfect commentary on Sydney's life, John thought. "Sydney, you need to relax more."

He could almost feel her stiffen beside him. "I'm perfectly happy with my life," she said.

Oops. Better steer clear of that subject. "I'm sorry. I didn't mean that to sound like a criticism."

"I know exactly what you meant."

John glanced at her rigid profile, then lapsed into silence. Better to keep his mouth shut, he decided, because it was obvious that anything he said was going to be misinterpreted. Somehow, during the course of the evening, he had done something to distance her, and until he figured out what it was, he was better off saying nothing.

She stared straight ahead for the remainder of the ride. He was glad it was short.

When they reached her building, she said, "You can just pull into the turnaround in front and drop me off. Save you having to park."

John almost agreed. After all, that would probably be best. Drop her off. Write her off.

And then he looked at her tense face, the tautness of her shoulders, the way she wouldn't look directly at him, and knew he couldn't leave with things like this between them. He had alienated her in some way, and he had to make things right.

"I thought you promised me the view from your patio," he said softly.

For the first time since they'd left the restaurant, she looked directly at him. Although it was too dark in the car to know for sure, John thought he saw a questioning flicker in the depths of her eyes.

"And I'm holding you to that promise," he added.

Without another word, he pulled into the garage.

Sydney's mind reeled in confusion.

Why had he insisted on coming up? If he thought

she was so boring and one-dimensional, why did he want to spend even one more minute in her company? As they stood outside her condo door, she fumbled with her keys.

"Here," John said behind her. "Let me." He took the keys from her and opened her door.

"Thanks." She didn't look at him. Why didn't he just go home and leave her alone? She dumped her purse on the coffee table. "The patio door is unlocked if you want to go outside." Realizing how chilly she sounded, she forced herself to turn around and inject a friendly note into her voice. "Can I bring you something? Coffee? Brandy? Or how about some Bailey's?"

Yes, that was it. Cheerful, friendly, completely nonchalant. Two could play at this game, she decided. She'd be the perfect hostess, even if it killed her.

He turned, giving her a smile. His eyes held a curious light. "Bailey's sounds nice."

"Bailey's it is." As she poured their drinks at the bar, she heard him open the patio door and walk outside. Muted sounds of the traffic below drifted into the room. Sydney used the few moments to gather together her shredded confidence. She told herself she didn't care one way or the other what John thought of her. So he'd disappointed her because she'd thought he was different. So what? She'd been wrong before.

She pasted a smile on her face and a few minutes later, two small crystal glasses of Bailey's in her hands, she walked out to join him on the patio. He was standing at the railing, the lights of downtown winked in the distance, and spread out around them like a carpet of diamonds was suburban Houston.

"Here you go." She handed him his drink, then stood a few inches away from him.

He smiled his thanks and took a sip.

She took a sip of hers. The smooth liqueur slid down her throat and warmed her. *I'm okay,* she thought. *I can do this.*

"I never thought I'd like this kind of living, but I can see its appeal," he said, turning sideways to face her.

She started to say this kind of living wasn't her idea of heaven, either, then thought, *Why bother? He doesn't really care what I think. All of his pretense at listening and understanding were just that—a pretense. A way to humor his client. No more. No less.* So all she did was nod and take another sip of her drink.

After a few moments of silence, John leaned over and set his glass on her small wrought-iron patio table. Then he turned and faced her again. He touched her arm. Turning her gently, he placed his hands on her shoulders and said, "Sydney, what's wrong?"

"I don't know what you mean," she said stiffly. She couldn't meet his eyes.

"You know exactly what I mean." With his right hand, he tipped her chin up.

He looked into her eyes for a long moment. Sydney's heart skipped a beat. She couldn't have spoken if her life had depended on it.

Wordlessly, he took her glass and placed it on the tabletop beside his. With the gentlest of touches, he placed his hands on either side of her face. "I wish I knew what I did or said that hurt your feelings or made you angry. Whatever it was, I'm sorry. I wouldn't hurt you for the world.''

Sydney swallowed. To her mortification, she could feel tears forming at the backs of her eyes, and it made her furious with herself. "Just forget it," she said.

"I can't forget it. You've been distant since the middle of dinner, and for the life of me, I can't figure out why."

For the life of her, Sydney couldn't think what to say. She sure wasn't going to admit what it was he'd said that had wounded her so deeply. She just nodded and said, "Don't worry about it. It's okay."

"It's not okay." His eyes searched hers.

Oh, God, don't keep looking at me like that!

"Sydney…" With the pad of his thumb, he brushed her lower lip.

Sydney trembled, closing her eyes. His touch set off a yearning so deep, so profound, her entire body ached. Suddenly, all the slights, all the hurts, all the pain of the past closed in on her, and she felt like one big, inadequate, needy mess. The only thought in her mind was a prayer that she get through what was left of this evening without making a fool of herself.

And then he kissed her.

When she felt his lips on hers, her eyes snapped open, her breath caught and her heart shot up into her throat, even though the kiss was as light as the brush of a feather.

He lifted his head and his gaze locked with hers. They stared at each other for a long moment, then he kissed her again, this time more firmly. This kiss caused an explosion of feeling so intense, Sydney shivered from the force of it. His hands tightened, and one slid around and under her hair to cup the back of her head.

He deepened the kiss, and Sydney's head spun. He nudged her mouth open, slipping his tongue inside, and once he'd gained entry, he claimed her fully.

His kiss produced all the old clichés. Fireworks. Crashing cymbals. Shooting stars. A dizzying array of sensations and emotions that made her bones melt and her head whirl.

As the kiss intensified, he pulled her tightly against him. Because she was so tall, they fit together perfectly, and she could feel his arousal against her, at almost the exact point where her own body pulsed in counterpoint.

Sydney forgot everything.

She forgot that her feelings had been hurt.

She forgot that she was no good at relationships and no good at sex.

She forgot that she never rushed into anything, that she never made decisions or acted based on her emotions.

Instead, she wrapped her arms around John, and as the cool autumn night surrounded them, she unlocked the gate that guarded her heart and let him claim that, too.

He kissed her again and again, until finally, by some kind of unspoken message, they slowly drew apart. Sydney felt weak and light-headed and totally bemused.

"What are we going to do about this, Sydney?" John said. He sounded as shaken as she felt.

She didn't pretend to misunderstand. Coy wasn't in her nature. "What would you like to do about it?"

He looked deep into her eyes. "I'd like to make love to you."

The words lingered in the air between them. All sorts of thoughts flitted through her mind in the space of a couple of seconds. Uppermost was the depth of her need—a need she hadn't acknowledged in a very long time.

"That's what I'd like, too," she said.

John drew her into his arms and kissed her again. His hands roamed her back, and everywhere they touched, she felt the heat of the passion building between them. If Sydney had had even the tiniest doubt, this kiss dispelled it. Being in John's arms, having him kiss her and hold her and touch her—all felt so right to her.

It didn't matter that she'd only been with him a total of three times. It didn't matter that she might be sorry tomorrow. It didn't even matter that *he* might be sorry tomorrow.

At this moment, she needed him, she wanted him and she trusted him.

When the slow kiss ended, John took her hand, and silently, they walked inside. Sydney's heart was beating too fast, and she felt disembodied, as if someone else were inhabiting her skin and she had floated off somewhere.

As John turned to shut the door behind them, from far below, the wail of an ambulance sounded through the clear night. For one second, Sydney wondered if the sound was an omen, a warning.

Then she shoved the thought from her mind. She didn't care. Tonight, she would forget all caution. Tonight, she would simply feel. Tonight, she would simply be.

The bedroom was flooded with moonlight. As they entered, the logistics of it all suddenly assailed Sydney, and she felt awkward and weird.

Why was it that in movies and books, people always seemed to find it so easy to get around the embarrassing details of undressing and birth control and actually getting in bed together?

In real life, these things certainly took the edge off a person's desire and made her wonder if she really knew what she was doing.

Maybe she *was* crazy.

Maybe this was a stupid idea.

Maybe she should at least wait until she'd known John longer.

But Sydney knew the amount of time she'd known John wasn't what was really bothering her. No, what was really bothering her was that she wasn't any good at sex. He was bound to be disappointed in her, and then . . . oh, God, it didn't bear thinking about.

"What's wrong?" John said. "Are you having second thoughts?" He lifted her hair and kissed the back of her neck, and Sydney shuddered. "If you are," he murmured, "say so."

She took a deep breath, then thought, *Oh, what the hell.* "No, I-I'm not having second thoughts, but there's, uh, something you should know."

His lips found the sensitive spot right behind her ear. "What?" he whispered.

Sydney could hardly talk for the shivery sensation that radiated from the point where his tongue met her skin to every corner of her body. "I-I'm not...not very good at this."

"Not very good at what?" His hands crept around to cover her breasts.

Sydney arched in response, a groan escaping her lips.

He laughed softly, then turned her to face him. Her breasts tingled from where he'd touched them. He cupped her face and kissed the tip of her nose.

"Sydney, we're not going to run a race or argue a case. We're going to make love." His eyes gleamed in the moonlight. "And so far, you're doing just fine." He kissed her slowly, trailing his mouth across her lips and cheeks, while his hands stroked her back and head. "I want you," he said. "Do you want me?"

She swallowed. She wanted him. She wanted him a lot. But she was terrified. What if she was an abysmal failure? "Y-yes, but it's been a long—"

John held her close for a moment and whispered against her hair. "It's been a long time for me, too."

Somehow, after that, everything was easier.

They didn't talk, just silently began to undress. When Sydney struggled with her back zipper, John said, "Here, let me."

Sydney closed her eyes and a tremor slid through her as he slowly pulled the zipper down. "Thanks," she murmured. Keeping her back to him, she finished removing her dress, her slip, then her stockings and pumps.

Shyness attacked her again once she'd gotten down to her panties and bra. When she finally got up the nerve to turn around, she saw that John, too, had stripped down to his briefs. There was enough light in the room for her to see that he had a great-looking body—not muscle-bound, which was a turnoff, as far as Sydney was concerned, but nicely proportioned and athletic-looking with just enough muscle definition to be attractive.

She wondered if he found her body attractive. She knew she wasn't lush and sexy, like some women, but her body was firm, and even though her breasts were small, she thought they were adequate. Still, he might like women who had fuller figures, sexier figures. Well, there wasn't anything she could do about that now. Or ever, she thought with a flash of humor. She took a deep breath. *What you see is what you get.*

He looked at her and grinned. "Who'd have thought it?" he said, and she heard the amusement in his voice. "Lace underwear. My, my, my." The amusement had been replaced with a husky edge.

Sydney blushed, and for the second time in less than a week, she was glad of the darkness. She knew most people would react the same way John had reacted if they saw the kind of underwear she favored. Just about every pair of panties and every bra she owned— except for her sports bra—was filmy and lacy and was usually a shade of violet or red or blue. It was her one secret concession to her femininity.

John sat on the edge of the bed. "Come here," he said.

Sydney swallowed. The feeling that someone else was inhabiting her body returned. Heart pounding, she walked toward him. When she got close enough, he reached for her and turned her around, his hands on her hips. Then he pulled her down onto his lap, nestling her close. His body felt warm and solid and very male.

He slid his hands around to cup her breasts again, and at this intimate touch with the only barrier between them the sheer fabric of her bra, Sydney gasped.

His warm mouth against her hair, he murmured, "Do you like that?" His thumbs rotated gently.

Her breasts blossomed under his touch, and a bittersweet longing filled her. "Yes," she managed to say, throwing her head back as his mouth sought her neck, then her ear. His tongue traced her earlobe.

Her heart galloped madly, and desire tore through her as he continued to caress her. Her breathing grew ragged.

"Spread your legs," he whispered. When she did, his right hand trailed down, slipping under the lace band of her panties and delving into the warm, wet recess that cried out for his touch. Sydney groaned as his fingers probed. She tensed against the onslaught of sensation.

Against her bottom, she felt his arousal, and the combination of his fingers moving inside her, his other hand continuing to caress her breasts and his hard body close up against her, shot her to the very edge of a climax she knew was going to be shattering. She fought against letting herself go and tried to pull away, but John held her firmly, his fingers insistent as they moved faster and with more pressure.

"Go with it," he whispered against her ear.

"No, I . . . wait—"

And then she came apart. "Yes," he said. "Yes." He held her tightly as her body convulsed, continuing to intensify her pleasure, until she was finally still and trembling with aftershock. Then he loosened his hold and with unsteady hands, unhooked her bra.

Moments later, rid of the last barriers between them, they pulled the covers down and climbed into Sydney's bed. He encircled her with his arms, throwing one leg over her and pulling her close. He felt hard and hot, and she reached down to touch him.

As her palm closed around him, he groaned, and the sound made Sydney feel bold. She gently moved her hand, and with a ragged growl, he rolled her over and positioned himself on top of her. "I can't wait," he muttered, spreading her legs.

Sydney lifted herself to give him easier access, and he eased inside. She sucked in her breath at the feeling, and as her body adjusted to absorb him, she wrapped her legs around him.

They began to move together, and with each thrust, John sank deeper into her. The heat and weight of him filled her, and that yearning, that need, that emptiness that needed filling, was suddenly assuaged.

Sydney clutched him tightly as their breathing accelerated and they strained harder. She could feel herself nearing another climax, and before she could stop it, it claimed her in wave after wave of intense pleasure. As her muscles contracted, John made a gutteral sound, and then, with one last mighty thrust, he spilled his lifeforce into her.

"I never even asked you about birth control," he said later. His finger traced her collarbone as she lay contented in his arms.

"I take birth control pills," she admitted. Then she chuckled. "Hope springs eternal, you know."

He laughed, too. Then, amusement still laced through his voice, he said, "I don't know why you thought you weren't any good at sex." His teeth nipped at her ear. "You're a pretty hot number."

Sydney laughed. "Oh, yeah, sure."

When he spoke again, the amusement was gone. He stroked her cheek. "You're not sorry, are you?"

"No! *Y-you're* not sorry, are you?"

His arms tightened around her. "No," he whispered fiercely. "What happened between us tonight is the best thing that's happened to me in a very long time."

Chapter Seven

John kissed Sydney goodbye and left for home at about three o'clock in the morning. Although Emily and Jeffrey were spending the night at his mother's house and he could have stayed all night at Sydney's, for the sake of his kids, he didn't want to chance any neighborhood gossip.

In particular, John wanted to avoid the scrutiny of old eagle-eyed Nathan McCroskey, who lived next door. The nosy old man was retired and got up at the crack of dawn. He knew everything that happened on their end of the street, and since he didn't have much else to do, he loved to talk. John had been the recipient of several juicy tidbits over the years, whether he wanted to hear them or not. Nathan never paid any attention when John tried to deter him; he just kept talking.

John could imagine the raised eyebrows on the old man's face if he should spy John coming in after an obvious overnight stay somewhere other than his home.

Not that John cared personally. But it was different when you had kids. If, and when, he brought someone else into their lives, he wanted to be the one to tell them.

As John drove home, he examined his feelings. The night's events had shaken him. He hadn't planned on or expected to make love to Sydney. In fact, his plans had been just the opposite. He'd told himself they would go out to dinner, pass a friendly, pleasant evening, and then he would take her home, and that would be it.

Finis.

He laughed at how he'd lied to himself.

No matter that things had just seemed to happen, to snowball once they'd gotten started, and he'd felt powerless to stop them. In his heart, he'd wanted them to happen, and he knew it.

Yet he had never imagined he would feel this way about her. Hell, he hadn't expected to *ever* feel this way again. He'd thought his capacity for this type of deep feeling had died along with Andrea.

Damn, things were complicated now. And there was no way to uncomplicate them. There would be no walking away, not now, not after last night. Somehow, he and Sydney would just have to play this thing through until the end.

Yeah, that was the crux of the problem.

The end.

And that's what worried him. Because when their relationship played itself out to its inevitable conclusion, and they went their separate ways, it would not be easy to forget Sydney.

And go their separate ways they would. Because he knew without being told that he and Sydney wanted different things out of life.

Despite all of this, John wasn't sorry they'd made love.

He couldn't help smiling as he remembered what it had been like. She was wonderful. So sweet, so willing, so responsive, yet so obviously inexperienced. And although he knew he wasn't her first lover, he also knew that in all the ways that counted, Sydney was untouched.

Untouched and very vulnerable.

And that, more than anything else, scared the hell out of him.

Sydney didn't hear from John on Sunday, and although she told herself she hadn't expected to, a nagging disappointment refused to go away. She spent most of the day working, and then, late in the afternoon, dropped in at her parents' house for about thirty minutes.

Her father wanted to hear everything that had happened that week. She gave him a rundown on the past few days in court, then said her goodbyes and left for home. She tried not to get her hopes up, yet a spark of anticipation fluttered inside as she walked into the condo.

She headed straight for the telephone and her answering machine. The red light wasn't blinking.

There were no messages.

Sighing, she sank onto a chair.

What if he was sorry? He'd said he wasn't, but what if he was, now that he'd had some time to think about everything?

What if I never hear from him again?

She shook herself. She would not think such negative thoughts.

But they refused to go away. For the rest of the evening, as she listlessly prepared a frozen dinner, as she tried to concentrate on the next day's proceedings, as she prepared for bed, the thought kept worming its way into her consciousness.

What if I never hear from him again?

And then, at ten o'clock, when she'd just gotten into bed and picked up a book, hoping she could read herself into sleep, the phone at her bedside rang.

Heart in her throat, she snatched the receiver up. "Hello?"

"Sydney? Hi. It's John."

A sweet joy spiraled through her. "Hi."

"Is it too late to be calling?"

"Oh, no. No, of course not."

"What were you doing?"

"I, well..." She laughed self-consciously. "I'm in bed with a book."

He was silent for a moment, then he chuckled. His voice was low and intimate as he said, "I wish you were in bed with me."

A delicious shiver snaked through her. "I—I do, too."

"I thought about you all day."

Oh, John, John. "Me, too." Sydney snuggled deeper into her pillows. She closed her eyes. She could almost feel him at the other end of the line. She could almost feel his hands, his breath, his kiss. A fierce desire flooded her, its intensity almost scary.

"What did you do today?" he said.

She told him about her day. "What did you do?"

"First I took the kids to church, then we had brunch with my mother and sister and her husband."

"That sounds nice."

"That was just the beginning. After brunch, Emily wanted to go to a movie with a friend, so I drove them over to the Galleria and then I took Jeffrey to get some new athletic shoes. Do you have any idea how expensive designer athletic shoes are?"

"I know how expensive *mine* are."

"Do you wear Air Jordans?"

Sydney laughed. "Not in this lifetime."

"Believe me, his new shoes will probably bankrupt me."

"Why did you buy them, then?" Sydney said without thinking. As soon as the words were out of her mouth, she realized they must sound like a criticism. "I'm sorry," she hurriedly added.

"It's okay. Before I had kids, I would've said the same thing."

"So after the shoe shopping, did you finally get to go home and rest?"

"We came home, but the word *rest* isn't in a single parent's vocabulary," John said wryly. "We tossed a football around for a while, then we came in and watched the Oilers game."

"Aha! So you *did* get to put your feet up."

"Yeah, eventually. Anyway, now the kids are finally in bed, so I called you."

"Is that the way your Sundays usually go?" Sydney wondered what it would be like to be part of a family unit like John's.

"Pretty much."

Sydney searched her mind for something to say. Some of her pleasure in his call had faded because he'd reminded her of the differences in their lives. In their worlds. In their futures.

"I kept wishing you were with us today, though," he said.

"You did?" She smiled.

"Maybe some Sunday, after your case is over, we can all spend the day together."

"I'd like that." Sydney was thrilled. He wasn't sorry about last night. He'd been thinking about her. He wanted her to spend time with him and his children.

"Do you like the zoo?" he asked.

"I don't know. I-I've never been to the zoo."

"Never been to the zoo? Not even as a kid?"

"No, not even as a kid."

"What kinds of things *did* you do when you were a kid?"

"Well, my father took me hunting with him. And horseback riding."

John didn't comment for a few seconds, and Sydney wondered what he was thinking. Finally, he said, "Well, I guess I'd better let you get some sleep. Big day tomorrow, right?"

"Yes."

"I'll call you tomorrow night, okay?"

"Yes."

After she gently replaced the receiver, Sydney lay there for a long time and replayed the conversation over and over in her mind.

And when she finally fell asleep, there was a smile on her face.

When Sydney returned to her office at five o'clock Monday afternoon, Norma gave her an odd, speculative sort of look.

Sydney frowned. "What's wrong?"

"Oh, nothing," Norma said, but she got up and followed Sydney into her office.

Sydney stopped dead.

A dozen delicate blush pink roses sat in a sparkling vase on top of her desk. Shock vaulted through her. *John.* She walked over to the desk and lifted the accompanying card from its holder. She tore open the little white envelope. It read:

Good luck this week. I can't wait to see you again.

John

It was the first time in her entire life that anyone had ever sent her flowers. The gift and the message on the card made her feel giddy with pleasure.

Behind her, Norma cleared her throat.

Without turning, Sydney said, "Did you want something, Norma?" She was amazed that her voice sounded so normal when she felt anything but.

"Here are some messages for you," Norma said.

Sydney finally turned, hoping her face would not betray her inner elation. She took the messages from Norma's outstretched hand.

Norma smiled, her green eyes bright. "The flowers are beautiful," she said.

Sydney nodded. "Yes, they are nice, aren't they?"

"Is it a special occasion?"

Sydney gave her secretary a look meant to quell—if not her curiosity—at least her questions. "Not that I know of."

Norma's mouth twitched.

Sydney wondered if the woman had X-ray eyes. No, that was ridiculous. How could she have any idea what the flowers meant or who they were from?

After Norma left the room, Sydney lifted the vase and buried her face in the fragrant blossoms. Tenderness and warmth flooded her. It was incredibly sweet of him to send her the flowers. She allowed herself a little while longer to savor the pleasure of the moment, then sighed and replaced the vase on her desk.

She still had a lot of work to do before she could call it a day. Remembering the messages Norma had given her, she rifled through them.

Then, for the second time that day, she froze.

The last message said: *John Appleton called at four-thirty. He wondered if his flowers had arrived. I told him they had.* Then there was a drawing of a smiley face, followed by Norma's name.

John decided he wanted to hear Sydney give her final argument on the Montgomery case. He talked to her on Tuesday night, and during the conversation she said she expected to give it the following day. He decided then and there that he would go.

Early Wednesday morning he called Pete Winsen, the bailiff for Judge Andrews's court. Pete was an old friend from John's law school days when John had worked as an unpaid assistant in Judge Macklin's court, which was across the hall from Judge Andrews's.

"Pete, this is John Appleton."

"Hey, John, how's it goin'?"

They talked for a few minutes, then John said, "I want to hear the final arguments in the Montgomery case. I understand it's standing-room-only. Can you get me in?"

"Yeah, sure I can. Lemme think. Whyn't you wait outside the judge's chambers at noon, and as soon as Judge Andrews goes to lunch, I'll let you in the back door. How's that sound?"

"Great. Thanks, Pete."

At eleven minutes past twelve, the door leading directly into Judge Andrews chambers opened, and the judge walked out. He nodded to John, and John nodded back. A few minutes later, the door opened again, and Pete, a burly ex-cop who'd had to quit the force because of a leg injury, beckoned him inside with a conspiratorial grin.

"I oughtta sell these seats," he said. "This is the most popular case on the dockets right now."

"I owe you one," John said.

John followed Pete through chambers and into the now-empty courtroom.

"What's your interest?" Pete said.

"The plaintiff's attorney is a friend of mine."

"Really? Sydney the Shark?" Pete made a face. "I didn't think she had any friends."

John resisted the impulse to jump to Sydney's defense. Better not to get into a discussion of Sydney.

"Thanks again," he said as he took a seat in the back row. He didn't want Sydney to know he was there. Although he had no delusions about making her nervous, he didn't want to distract her in any way.

At one twenty-five, the double doors leading into the courtroom opened, and a crowd of people hurried in, scrambling to get seats. John noticed dozens of press badges and cameras. Yeah, it was a three-ring circus, all right, just as he'd imagined. When even the walls were lined with people, Pete turned away the spectators pushing for entry at the doorway.

A tall man with a pockmarked face protested. "Why'd he get in and not me?"

"Them's the breaks," Pete said, firmly closing the doors in the man's face.

John watched as first the jury, then the legal teams of each side filed in. He felt an unfamiliar stirring of proprietary pride as Sydney, looking preoccupied, walked in. She wore a dark gray suit and white blouse and looked every inch the competent attorney. She didn't look around the courtroom, so John needn't have worried about her spotting him. She *did* turn around and speak to a blond woman sitting directly behind the plaintiff's table, and John wondered who the woman was.

When Judge Andrews entered the courtroom a few minutes later, the rumble of conversation stopped almost immediately, which didn't surprise John. Welton Andrews had a reputation for being crotchety, at least where spectators were concerned, and he'd been known to throw everyone out if they disrupted the proceedings in any way.

Ten minutes later, the afternoon session began. After the judge's instructions to the jury, he turned to Sydney and said, "Miss Wells? Are you ready to present your argument?"

"Yes, Your Honor, I am." Sydney stood, and John noticed she held nothing in her hands. That didn't surprise him, either. Even knowing her the short time he'd known her, he'd realized Sydney was not the kind of attorney who would need notes. Her arguments would be memorized and presented with no hesitation and no need for reminders.

She walked slowly toward the jury, her movements measured and controlled. She stood looking at the twelve men and women, letting her gaze go from one end of the jury box to the other.

The courtroom was very still, as if the crowd held its collective breath, knowing the show that was coming would be a good one.

"Ladies and gentlemen," Sydney began, her voice deceptively soft, "for the past week and a half, we've listened to doctors and psychiatrists, social workers and friends of both the McKinseys, Kara Montgomery's foster parents, and Shanna Montgomery, her birth mother. We've also heard Kara herself tell us how she feels about her life and the way she wants to live it. We've heard hours of testimony, a lot of it wrenching and emotional. We've seen Shanna Montgomery cry and we've heard her torment as she begged for the chance to raise her daughter. We've also seen the goodness and caring in the McKinseys and the way Kara loves them, and the way they love her. We've seen the bonding between them, and the trust."

She paused, looking at them intently. "Our emotions have been on a roller coaster, haven't they? Even I, who represent Kara and her bid to stay with the only real parents she's ever known, have felt sympathy for Shanna Montgomery. Who wouldn't feel sympathy for Shanna Montgomery when she so eloquently told us how empty she feels without her daughter? Who wouldn't feel her agony and her desperation as she described the frustration of not being able to give Kara the kind of home she deserves? Who wouldn't wonder if maybe Kara *should* be with her birth mother, especially after Shanna's last plea was for all of us to understand that no matter what Kara thinks she wants, she *belongs* to Shanna?"

Here she paused again, and John knew the crucial moment was coming. Just as a symphony built to a crescendo, or a book built to its resolution, so a good attorney built to the climax of his or her argument.

Sydney faced the jury squarely. Her voice rang out with conviction. "Ladies and gentlemen of the jury, I thought about that last statement of Shanna Montgomery's, when she said Kara *belonged* to her. I thought about it and thought about it, and I'm here to tell you today that that statement is the most revealing thing Shanna Montgomery said to us. If Shanna Montgomery really loved Kara the way she claims to, if she really had Kara's best interests at heart, she would never have said Kara belonged to her. Because, ladies and gentlemen, no one *belongs* to anyone else. Kara Montgomery is a person, not a piece of property. For too long, our society has treated children as if they were chattel instead of people with rights.

"Kara is an intelligent ten-year-old girl who has just as many rights as you or I do. She knows how she feels, and she knows with whom she wants to live. She is not a piece of property to be bartered over or sold. Shanna Montgomery has always treated Kara as her possession, and I'm afraid she always will. When it was inconvenient to keep her, she tossed her away, and now that her circumstances have changed, she wants Kara back.

"I say Shanna forfeited the right to her child years ago. I say Kara's rights supersede any that Shanna might still have. I say that in your hearts you must know this, too. Be brave, ladies and gentlemen. The easy choice would be to deny Kara her petition. To force her to return to her mother. The right decision is harder. But I have confidence in you. I think you'll make that hard decision. I think you'll show the world that you agree with me, that our children must be accorded the same rights as the adults in this country enjoy.

"Please, ladies and gentlemen, do it. Do what you know is right in your heart. Show Kara that you respect her as a person. Show her that she has more value than a television set or a piece of land. Let her divorce her birth mother, and allow her to remain with the parents she loves."

John could almost hear Sydney's sigh before she ended with, "Thank you," and walked briskly back to her seat.

There was a rustle and buzz in the courtroom before the judge rapped his gavel smartly and said, "Quiet!"

The buzz subsided.

"Mr. Randall?" the judge said.

Rick Randall, the attorney representing Shanna Montgomery, stood. John knew Rick Randall slightly and knew that he was commonly referred to as Slick Rick because he so often managed to win difficult cases. He was a talented speaker with considerable acting skills, a real asset in the courtroom. He also had an all-American look, and John knew juries liked him. Today he wore a gray suit and light blue shirt with a dark blue tie.

He paced in front of the jury box, smiling at each juror as he did. John looked at Sydney. She was listening to something her assistant was saying to her.

Rick Randall cleared his throat. "Ladies and gentlemen, despite what my esteemed colleague has said to you, the fact remains that Shanna Montgomery is

Kara Montgomery's mother. Lottie McKinsey is not. And George McKinsey is not Kara's father.''

He shrugged. ''Those are the facts. Another fact is that the McKinseys made a promise. A sworn, written promise when they became foster parents. A promise they want you to conveniently forget. That promise was that they would never attempt to keep, on any kind of permanent basis, any of the children they contracted to care for. That they fully understood that these children were only in their custody *temporarily*. They signed that statement, ladies and gentlemen, before witnesses. They took a solemn oath, just as you all did when you became jurors, and now... now...they want to pretend that oath was never made.

''And why?'' Rick Randall turned around and pointed his index finger directly at the McKinseys. ''I'll tell you why! Because Lottie and George McKinsey have changed their minds. That's why. They've changed their minds, and they want to renege on their promise.'' He turned again to face the jury.

''Because we all know, ladies and gentlemen, that the plaintiff's attorney can say this suit was brought about solely because Kara Montgomery wants it, but I maintain—and I know you all would agree with me—that a ten-year-old girl would never come up with the idea of divorcing her mother unless that idea was planted in her head.

''Do we really want to allow the McKinseys to adopt Kara? A couple who would swear to one thing and do another? Do we really want to penalize a mother who, through no fault of her own, had to give her child over to other people's care temporarily? Is that the message we want to send the world? That if a woman does the right thing, gives her child over to the temporary custody of the state, that when the time comes when she *can* care for her daughter, she will be denied?

"Do we want the world to believe that the state of Texas rewards liars and punishes those who are truthful? My esteemed colleague would have us believe that Kara Montgomery has certain rights. I agree. She, like all other children, has the right to security, food, a place to live, someone to watch over her and freedom from abuse and cruelty. Her mother made sure those rights were taken care of. I don't think, however, that Kara Montgomery, or any other ten-year-old child, has the right to make decisions like this one. There's a reason children aren't allowed to vote or serve in armies or work in factories. The reason is, they are children. They do not have either the physical or emotional maturity to make their own decisions.

"Why, if we allowed our children to make all their own decisions, we know exactly what they would be, don't we? They would decide they didn't want to go to school, they didn't want to eat their green beans, and—when crossed—that they didn't want to live with their parents anymore."

Rick Randall made a scoffing sound, and his meaning was clear to everyone in the courtroom, John was sure. "This is ridiculous, ladies and gentlemen. Neither Kara Montgomery nor any other child under the age of eighteen should be allowed to decide how and where they want to live.

"There is only one right decision in this case. I know it, and you know it. Return Kara Montgomery to her rightful place—with her mother, Shanna."

He smiled at the jurors. "Thank you. You've been a wonderful jury."

A bravura performance, John thought. But he thought Sydney had done an excellent job, as well. Now the jury would decide.

Although John had planned to leave without talking to Sydney, as he moved toward the exit along with the other spectators, Sydney looked in his direction, and their gazes met.

Even from this distance, he saw the flush of pleasure on her cheeks, the surprised light in her eyes. He smiled and raised his hand in greeting. She smiled back. The blond woman he'd noticed earlier was standing alongside Sydney, and as John worked his way through the crowd to where they stood, he realized how much the two women resembled each other.

"John," Sydney said as he came within speaking distance, "I had no idea you were here. You never said you planned to come."

"I just decided last night." He wanted to lean over and kiss her cheek, but contented himself with taking her hand and squeezing it.

"John, I want you to meet my sister, Claire Stevens. Claire, this is John Appleton, a friend of mine."

"Hello, John." Claire Stevens held out her hand to shake his. "It's nice to meet you."

"It's nice to meet you, too," he said. Claire wasn't as tall as her sister, but she had the same intense blue eyes and her face was the same shape as Sydney's. He noticed that she looked him over curiously.

"Sydney did a wonderful job, I thought," Claire said.

"I agree."

Sydney smiled. "I hope the jury agrees."

"I hope you don't have to wait too long to find out," Claire said.

"Actually," Sydney said, "the longer we have to wait, the better it will be for us." Her gaze met John's.

"You're right," he said.

"Why is that?" Claire asked, looking at him.

"It's just as Sydney said," John answered. "The easy decision would be to deny Kara's request. The harder one would be to grant it. Harder decisions always take longer."

"So what are you going to do now?" Claire asked.

"Go back to the office and wait, I guess." Sydney's gaze met John's again.

The three of them walked out of the courtroom together. Once they reached the main floor of the Family Law Center, Claire said, "Well, I parked across the street, so I guess I'll say goodbye." She and Sydney hugged, then Claire turned to John. "I hope I see you again sometime."

"I hope so, too."

Once she was gone, he took Sydney's arm, and they exited the building together. The November day was bright and warmer than it had been for weeks. "Did you drive over?" John asked.

"No, I walked."

"I'll walk back with you, if that's okay."

"But what about your car? Isn't it parked around here?"

"It won't kill me to walk both ways." He let go of her elbow and took her hand, lacing his fingers through hers. He smiled into her eyes. "I've missed you. I haven't seen you since Saturday night."

And then, completely ignoring the people on the street, and the fact that someone they knew might see them, and the fact that it was totally inappropriate and completely out of character for him to do so, he pulled her into his arms and kissed her.

Chapter Eight

The verdict came in on Thursday.

At two o'clock, Sydney got the call. Five minutes later, accompanied by the two other lawyers on her team, she was on her way.

Kara and the McKinseys were waiting for her in the hallway outside the courtroom. Photographers and reporters and dozens of spectators milled around.

Sydney's stomach felt queasy, but she maintained a calm facade. She squeezed Kara's shoulder. The little girl's big amber eyes looked scared.

Lottie and George McKinsey looked equally frightened.

Sydney took a deep breath as the jury filed in.

"Mr. Foreman, have you reached your verdict?" Judge Andrews asked.

The jury foreman said, "Yes, Your Honor, we have." He handed a slip of paper to the bailiff, who handed it to the judge. The judge read it impassively, nodded once, then handed it back to the bailiff.

The bailiff handed the paper back to the foreman, who opened it and said, "In the matter of Montgomery versus Montgomery, we the jury find in favor of the plaintiff, Kara Montgomery."

Cheers erupted at Sydney's table, and a babble of excited voices burst forth from the spectators.

"No!" shouted Shanna Montgomery. "No!" She lunged toward Kara, but her attorney grabbed her and held her back. "Kara!" she called, tears running down her face.

The McKinseys hugged Kara and each other, then, one on either side of Kara, came up to Sydney to thank her. Lottie McKinsey's pale blue eyes were filled with happy tears.

Relief made Sydney feel weak as she smiled and accepted their thanks. She stooped down. She and Kara hugged. "Be happy, Kara," she said.

"I'll miss you," Kara said. "Will you come and see me sometime?"

"I'll try," Sydney said, knowing she would never go. It was always best to make a clean break.

"Come on, Kara," Lottie said. "We have to go now."

Then the three of them were gone.

It was an hour before Sydney was able to get away from the reporters and return to her office.

When she got there, the office was abuzz.

"Congratulations, Miss Wells," Norma said. "And guess what? The producer of the *Geneva Ward Show* called and wants you to call her back." Awe and excitement filled her voice as she said the name of the popular syndicated talk show. "And your father called. Twice."

Sydney could care less about the talk show. She figured her father must have already heard about the verdict.

"I heard it on CNN," he said gleefully when she called him back. "Damn, I'm proud of you, Sydney. CNN! It's just as I told you. Everyone's going to know your name. Soon the sky will be the limit."

Sydney stopped herself before blurting out that she didn't care about all of that. She knew it would upset him if she admitted that fame wasn't her objective. He would probably have a heart attack if she told him about the *Geneva* show and that, if they had called to invite her to appear, she would turn the invitation down.

"The reporter said your argument was 'brilliantly conceived,'" her father continued. "His exact words were 'brilliantly conceived and the exact note to strike with the jury.'" He laughed triumphantly. "I can't wait to read what the *Chronicle* and the *Post* have to say."

The more her father talked, the more deflated Sydney felt, and if anyone had asked her why, she wouldn't have been able to answer.

"What's wrong?" her father said when he'd wound down. "Aren't you excited? Did something happen that you're not telling me?"

Sydney forced herself to answer brightly. "No, of course not. I'm just tired. I haven't been getting much sleep lately. And you know...the tension is finally over...."

"One good night's sleep is all you need," he said. "Boy, Sydney, didn't I *tell* you? By God, you *should've* been a man. You've got all the right stuff."

As her father's exuberance continued unabated, Sydney eyed the roses John had sent her. They were still fresh-looking, and their fragrance permeated the office. Something painful twisted inside her. "Dad," she interrupted. "I've got to go. I've got a lot of calls to return."

"Oh, sure, of course you do! Well, we can talk tonight. Since this case is really special, we're really gonna celebrate. I'm taking you to Tony's."

Her father and mother always took her out to dinner to celebrate her victories, and most of the time, Sydney enjoyed it. Today, though, for some reason, Sydney didn't feel the same enthusiasm she usually felt. The thought of going to Tony's, where all the movers and shakers of Houston liked to see and be seen, left her completely cold. Besides, what if John—?

She broke off the thought.

John had said nothing about taking her out tonight, although he had asked her to call him as soon as she knew the verdict.

She started to tell her father she might not be able to go out with him tonight, then thought better of it. He would want to know why, and how could she explain that she hoped John would ask her out? Her father didn't know anything about John, and she wasn't ready to tell him.

She said goodbye, then immediately called John's office. Their receptionist had returned from her vacation, and she answered the phone.

"I'll connect you with Mr. Appleton," she said after Sydney identified herself.

"Sydney! Is it in?" John said before she'd even said hello.

"Yes. We won."

"That's *great!* Congratulations."

"Thanks."

"Has the euphoria worn off yet?"

She laughed softly. "What are you, a mind reader?"

"It's not so hard to figure you out."

"I can't even figure me out. How'd you manage to do it?"

He chuckled. "I had you pegged from the very first time I set eyes on you, Counselor."

"Oh?" But she smiled, because she had a feeling he was right.

"The thing that drives you is the challenge. Once that's gone, there's bound to be a letdown. Only natural. Tell you what, why don't I get a sitter and we'll go out and celebrate tonight?" His voice deepened. "Better yet, we can order a pizza and celebrate at your place."

Sydney closed her eyes. There was nothing she wanted more than to spend the evening with John. Since yesterday, when he'd kissed her on the sidewalk in front of dozens of people, she'd dreamed of seeing him again, of making love with him again.

Regret filled her voice. "Oh, John, I wish I could, but my... my parents are taking me out."

"Oh, well..."

For one moment, she considered asking him to join them, but her feelings for him were too confused, too new and too fragile to put them out there for anyone else to see. Until she knew what place John would occupy in her life, she wasn't sure she wanted her family to know about him. Bad enough that Claire probably suspected something, but at least Claire would not question her or expect answers Sydney wasn't willing to give.

"I'm sorry," she said again. "It's just that it's a kind of tradition—"

"I understand. You don't owe me any explanations."

Sydney bit her lip. He sounded so distant. She wished she knew what to say. Oh, God, she was no good at this kind of thing!

"Maybe you could come over later?" she said.

"My sitter is a teenager, Sydney," John said in a patient voice, a you-should-know-better-than-to-suggest-this voice. "And it's a weeknight."

"Oh, of course." Her lack of knowledge about the practical aspects of having children were underscored everytime she talked to him. And they only emphasized the differences in their lives. She hoped desperately that he would suggest they see each other tomorrow night. Pride wouldn't allow her to.

"Listen," he said, "I've got another call, so I'd better go. Have fun tonight."

Sydney swallowed her disappointment and fought the urge to say something, anything, that would keep him on the line. "I will. Goodbye."

"Goodbye."

"Damn," she whispered after he'd hung up. "Damn." What should she have said or done differently? Maybe she should have said yes to John and called and canceled with her father.

But how could she do that? Her father would have been crushed. He'd looked forward to this for months, ever since Sydney had first told him about the case. He would never have understood. His feelings would have been hurt.

But she'd hurt John's feelings, she was sure of it. And after he'd made the effort to come to court to hear her give her final argument.

Sydney laid her head down on her arms. She hated feeling torn like this. Hated being in the middle of forces she wasn't sure she understood. Hated knowing she was such a complete dud at anything having to do with a relationship.

"What if I've screwed everything up with John?" she whispered.

Before she could even contemplate an answer, Norma buzzed her on the intercom. For the rest of the day, the phone calls of congratulations and invitations and requests for interviews came nonstop, and Sydney had no more time to think or to worry.

* * *

"You know, John, you're acting like a bear with a sore paw. What's wrong with you?"

John looked at his sister. "I'm sorry," he muttered.

"Are you angry about something?" Janet persisted.

"No."

"Did something happen that I should know about?"

"No."

"Well, *something's* wrong! It's just not like you to snap everybody's head off. You practically had Tammi in tears a few minutes ago."

John grimaced. "Dammit! Why does everyone have to be so damn sensitive?"

Janet gave him a long-suffering look—a look that was so exactly like Emily's when she was exasperated that John almost smiled. "And I don't appreciate your swearing, either," she said stiffly.

John heaved a loud sigh. "Okay, okay, you've made your point. I'll go apologize to Tammi. Will that make you happy?"

In answer, Janet just gave him a withering look, then she stalked off in the direction of her office.

A few minutes later, John walked into the reception area. "Tammi?" he said to their receptionist.

Tammi looked up. Her gray eyes held a wounded look.

"Janet said I hurt your feelings. I'm sorry. I wasn't mad at you. I had something on my mind, that's all."

"Well . . ." Suddenly, she smiled, her freckled face once more sunny. "It's okay, John."

Later, sitting in his office, he tried to figure out why he'd gotten so bent out of shape over Sydney's declining his invitation. He'd acted like one of the kids when they didn't get their way. Just because Sydney had already made plans didn't mean she hadn't wanted to be with him.

Careful, he cautioned himself. Remember, this relationship is only temporary. You're allowing it to assume too much importance in your life.

He wished now that he'd been nicer about it when Sydney had said she couldn't go out with him tonight. He hoped his churlishness hadn't spoiled her evening in any way.

Boy, you've sure got a swelled head! She's probably having a wonderful time and hasn't thought about you once.

The thought didn't make him feel any better.

Sydney had never spent a more miserable evening in her life. No matter what her father said or did, all she could think about was John.

"Sydney, I don't understand you," her father said over their chocolate soufflé, a Tony's specialty. "I thought you'd be ecstatic over this victory."

"Sid," her mother said, "maybe she's tired. Listening to you expound all night would make *me* tired."

Sydney's father didn't bat an eyelash at his wife's admonition. In fact, he acted as if he hadn't even heard her. "Sydney, this is what we've been waiting for," he continued. "This is our chance."

Sydney bit back the words she longed to say. Her father acted as if he'd had something to do with her victory today. *Well, didn't he? Isn't he the one who pushed you and encouraged you and believed in you? What's wrong with you? Why are you so ungrateful?* "Yes, Dad, I know. Mom's right. I *am* tired."

For the rest of the evening, she tried to wipe thoughts of John out of her mind. She tried to respond to her father's comments and questions with enthusiasm. And she promised herself that if John didn't call her tomorrow, she would call him.

"Sydney, Mr. Folger would like to see you in his office," said his secretary the following morning.

"Now?"

"Now."

Francis K. Folger was the managing partner of Folger & Hubbard, the grandson of the original founder of the firm. When he said jump, everyone in the firm jumped.

Sydney straightened her olive green suit jacket and ran a brush through her hair before exiting her office. Three minutes later, she stood outside Mr. Folger's office door while his secretary announced her.

The door opened. Brenda, his secretary, said, "You can go in now, Miss Wells."

"Sydney, my dear, come in," Francis Folger said, looking up from his massive oak desk. His dark eyes studied her as she walked toward him. "Have a seat."

She sat in one of the burgundy leather chairs grouped to the right side of his desk. Behind him, the glass faces of dozens of buildings that made up the Houston skyline glittered in the November sun.

"Congratulations on winning the Montgomery case," he said, smiling at her.

"Thank you." She tried to relax in her chair, but there was something about being summoned to Francis Folger's office that produced the same feelings of nervousness that a summons to a principal's office might produce in a recalcitrant student.

"I understand you're being assaulted by the media," Folger said.

Sydney smiled. "Yes, they have been rather relentless since the verdict came in. But that should die down soon...I hope."

"Brenda tells me you've been contacted by the *Geneva Ward Show*."

"Yes," she answered guardedly.

He tented his hands in front of him. "She also tells me you've refused an invitation to appear."

So that's what this was all about. "Yes, I have."

"May I ask why?"

Sydney chose her words carefully. "I don't see the point of rehashing the case on a talk show."

"Don't you? You disappoint me, Sydney."

Sydney stared at him.

"Would it make any difference to you if I told you I would very much like you to call them back and tell them you've changed your mind?"

Sydney swallowed. "You know it would."

Francis Folger smiled and leaned forward. "I was certain you'd see it my way."

* * *

A little after three that afternoon, Norma buzzed her on the intercom and said, "Miss Wells, Mr. Appleton is on line two." Sydney's heart went *zing,* and she realized that no matter how she'd tried to pretend differently, she'd been worried that he wouldn't call her.

Her hand actually trembled as she picked up the receiver. She wondered what John would think if he could see her.

"Hello, John," she said.

"Hi. Are you busy?"

"Not too busy to talk to you."

"Have things settled down since yesterday?"

"Yes, thank goodness. I don't think I'd like being a celebrity. Being hounded by reporters isn't much fun."

"Good for business, though."

"Yes." She thought about Francis Folger and his edict concerning the *Geneva* show.

"Did you have a good time last night?"

"It was nice." *I wish I'd been with you, instead.*

"Good. Now that the trial's over, do you think you might have some free time this weekend?"

Sydney smiled happily. "I've got a lot of free time this weekend."

"Good," he said again. "Do you like to dance?"

"Well . . ."

"Well what?"

"I like the *idea* of dancing, but I'm not a very good dancer."

"Is that your opinion, or did someone tell you that?"

"I didn't need anyone to tell me what is painfully obvious."

"Maybe you just need the right partner."

"Maybe I do."

"What about me?" His voice was light and teasing.

"What about you?" she countered, grinning.

"Do I fill the bill?"

She waited a couple of seconds before saying, "I think you probably fill the bill perfectly."

"I was hoping you'd say that."

John decided that dancing with Sydney was as close to being perfect as anything could be. Contrary to what she'd told him, she wasn't a bad dancer. In fact, he thought she was pretty good.

He had brought her to a favorite spot—a small Village club he and Andrea had frequented. The club featured a live band on Friday and Saturday nights. The band played mostly popular ballads from the forties, with a few more contemporary pieces interspersed throughout the evening.

He had wondered about bringing Sydney somewhere that held so many memories, but found it was okay. He didn't feel sad at all. The realization was bittersweet. Some part of him didn't want to let go of his past, even as the other part of him was reaching toward the future.

"This is nice," Sydney said, as they did a slow foxtrot.

"The club? Or dancing with me?" John pulled her closer and breathed in the jasmine scent she wore.

"Both."

He closed his eyes and enjoyed the sensation of her body moving against his. After a moment, he murmured in her ear, "When we get back to your place, it'll be even nicer."

"Is that a promise?" There was a funny little catch in her voice.

"It's definitely a promise."

For the rest of the evening, making love to Sydney was all John could think about. And he knew she felt the same way. Each time he looked into her eyes, he saw the awareness and the expectation. Finally, he said, "Let's go home."

"Yes," she said.

He drove too fast because he couldn't wait.

When they reached her condo, they barely made it inside the door before John hauled her into his arms and began kissing her greedily.

They undressed each other standing right there, and their lovemaking grew so frenzied they didn't make it to the bed before John was driving into her, listening to her moans and cries, which only fueled his desire.

When Sydney's body contracted around him, John exploded. He held her tightly, her legs locked around him, as pleasure assaulted him.

Afterward, while their breathing slowed and their bodies cooled, he held her close. He could feel her heart beating against his, and he stroked her slowly. He kissed her cheek. "I'm sorry I was so rough with you," he whispered.

Her hands tightened around him and she buried her face against his neck. Her warm breath feathered him as she said, "You weren't rough."

"I wasn't exactly gentle."

"We were in a hurry."

He chuckled. "Yes, I guess you could say that." He gently disentangled her, then propped himself up on one arm so he could look at her. Her eyes gleamed in the moonlight, and her skin looked like porcelain. He traced the curve of her jaw with his forefinger, then slowly trailed it down to her collarbone. "Let's go slow this time, okay?"

"This time?" she said, her voice husky.

He smiled, his hand closing over her breast. As he gently rubbed his thumb over the peak, he felt her quick intake of breath as it hardened into a tight little nub. "If you don't want to," he murmured, "just say the word. I'll stop."

She reached up and pulled his head down to meet her mouth. "If you do, I'll kill you," she whispered, and then they stopped talking entirely.

Much later, after Sydney had fallen asleep in his arms, John lay there and wondered what was going to happen to them. Making love to Sydney tonight, especially the second time, when it had been slower and he had been intent on giving her pleasure, had made him realize that he'd been lying to himself.

Not only would it not be easy to walk away from her when the time came to call it quits.

It would be one of the hardest things he'd ever had to do.

Chapter Nine

Since his children were away, John stayed the night, and the next morning they decided to drive to Galveston for the day, something Sydney hadn't done in years.

She wondered if she should call her parents and tell them she would not be coming by for dinner. She decided not to. After all, it wasn't as if she *had* to be there. If she didn't show up, they would assume she was working. She ignored the twinge of guilt as she pictured her father's disappointment. He was probably looking forward to hearing what was next on her agenda.

I don't care. For once, I'm going to do exactly what I want to do.

"Do you think it'll be cold?" she asked John, putting her family out of her mind.

"Yes. I'd wear something warm," he called from the patio. "It's windy, and it's bound to be even windier on the beach."

Sydney put on a favorite blue warm-up suit and her Reeboks.

Then they drove to John's house so he could change into casual clothes, too. Sydney went inside with him.

"Would you like to see the rest of the house?" he asked after he'd checked his office messages.

"I'd love to."

But once they were upstairs, and Sydney saw all the homey touches, all the evidence that a woman had lovingly chosen the furnishings and decorations, she was almost sorry she'd come up. And when he showed her his living room, the first thing she noticed was the silver-framed portrait sitting on top of a small cherrywood table. A laughing, redheaded woman with clear green eyes looked out from the frame.

Sydney knew the woman was Andrea.

John followed her gaze. Sydney watched as his face changed and softened. "My wife," he said.

Sydney nodded. "She was lovely."

"Yes." His gaze didn't meet Sydney's.

She swallowed. What was he thinking? Was he still in love with Andrea? Would he always be in love with her? Was he comparing Sydney to her?

Sydney knew in any comparison, she would probably come up short. How could she help it?

She could hear her father's oft-repeated assertion: *Sydney, you should have been a man,* and that old taunt from that old boyfriend, *Sydney, you're boring and one-dimensional.*

Was John thinking about how inadequate Sydney was? Wishing Andrea was here with him, instead? Suddenly, even their lovemaking seemed suspect. Was he just using her because he needed sexual gratification? All these thoughts, and dozens of others, whirled through her mind.

"Sydney."

She slowly looked up.

His dark gaze was thoughtful. "Come here."

Unable to resist his lure, she walked toward him. He opened his arms, cradled her head against his chest and stroked her hair.

"Andrea will always be a part of me," he said. "She was the mother of my children. And I loved her very much."

"I know." That was the trouble. She did know.

"But she's dead. And I'm finally getting over it, and a lot of that's due to you."

Sydney's heart beat faster.

He lifted her head and kissed her—a long, lingering kiss that set her pulse racing. Then he smiled and said, "Feel better?"

She nodded.

"Good. Now, if we're going to get to Galveston and back before the kids return, we'd better get started."

That evening, after a wonderful, lazy day of walking the beach, window-shopping on The Strand and eating fresh seafood at Gaido's, they headed home. As they drove north on the Gulf Freeway, Sydney said,

"I've been meaning to tell you—I'm flying to Chicago tomorrow afternoon."

"Oh? New case or something?"

"No, I, uh... I'm going to appear on the *Geneva Ward Show*."

She could see the surprise on his face. "You *are?* Because of the Montgomery case?"

"Yes. Stupid, isn't it?"

"Why do you say that?"

"I don't know. It's just that this thing has turned into a three-ring circus. I *hate* the idea of being on the show."

"If you hate it so much, then why are you doing it?"

"It's a command performance," she said, grimacing.

"Whose command?"

"Francis K. Folger, the fearless leader of Folger & Hubbard."

"I can see why he'd want you to do it. It's quite a coup." There was an undercurrent to his voice that gave Sydney a funny twinge. "When will the show air?" he continued. "Tuesday?"

"No. It'll be taped Tuesday morning and shown Wednesday. I think it comes on at four in Houston." When he said nothing, she added, "Will you watch?"

"I wouldn't miss it."

Somehow, his answer wasn't satisfying, but she couldn't have said why. She only knew she felt uneasy, and she wished she'd never brought up the subject.

* * *

John brought the nine-inch TV set he kept in his bedroom down to his office. At four o'clock Wednesday, he shut his office door and turned on the *Geneva* show.

The opening music was just fading.

"Last week," Geneva said, "a little girl in Houston, Texas, was granted a divorce from her mother. This case has stirred up a lot of controversy all over the country. Many people are frightened by this decision, feeling that, on a whim, their children could decide to divorce them."

She explained some of the details of the case, then went on to introduce all of her guests: Kara, the McKinseys, Sydney and two psychologists. Sydney had explained to John that Shanna Montgomery would appear via a remote camera—the only condition under which the McKinseys would permit Kara to be on the show.

John had mixed feelings about Sydney's appearance today. Part of him was proud of her and knew that an appearance such as this one was going to do big things for her career. The other part of him wondered what the hell he was doing getting tangled up with someone like her—a woman whose career path and future life-style was going to be completely opposite to the kind of life he had chosen for himself.

Even so, he was filled with admiration as he watched her. Sydney fielded questions from Geneva and then from the audience with aplomb, her replies logical and succinct. She seemed completely self-possessed and confident. Sometimes it was hard for John to reconcile this professional persona of hers to her personal, much more insecure self.

"How do you answer those critics who say what you did in the courtroom is going to set a disturbing precedent, one parents are right to be wary of?" Geneva asked Sydney.

"I say as long as parents accord their children respect, they have nothing to worry about," Sydney countered. "Perhaps those parents who consider their children possessions are right to be wary. Their children may not ever go to the extreme lengths Kara was forced to go, but they may cut their parents from their lives, nevertheless."

One of the psychologists interrupted. "I think Miss Wells has made an important point," he said. "When a child feels a lack of respect from his parent, he often distances that parent from his life when he becomes an adult."

He then turned to Sydney and asked her another question.

Just as Sydney began to answer, there was a knock on John's office door.

"John?" The door opened, and Janet walked in. "John, Kate MacAllister just called—" She stopped and stared at the screen. "Isn't that Sydney Wells?"

John nodded. "Yes."

"Is that the *Geneva* show?" Janet's voice had taken on a note of incredulity.

"Uh-huh."

"What's *she* doing there?"

"She was invited to appear because of the decision in the Montgomery case."

Janet gave him a blank look.

"Don't you ever read the newspaper?" John asked.

Janet shrugged. "I hate to read depressing things. You know that." She sat on the corner of his desk and watched for a while. Then, heaving a sigh, she stood and said, "Listen, about Kate Mac—"

"Can it wait, Jan? I'd like to hear the rest of this."

Janet frowned. "This is important, John."

"This is important, too."

Janet didn't answer for a few seconds, then, in a tight, disapproving voice, said, "You're seeing a lot of her, aren't you?"

John stiffened and told himself not to lose his temper. "Yes, I am," he said evenly, continuing to watch the show. Maybe she'd take the hint and leave his office. When long moments passed, and she didn't, he looked at her. "What's wrong?" He'd hoped to avoid another pointless discussion, but he could see his sister wouldn't be satisfied until she'd said her piece.

"*She's* what's wrong," Janet said, pointing to the screen.

"And just what do you mean by that crack?"

"Oh, come on, John. You know what I mean. She's all wrong for you."

"You don't know what you're talking about," John said. He willed her to leave the office. Drop the subject. He didn't want to discuss Sydney, and he was getting damned sick and tired of Janet's unsolicited advice.

What was wrong with her, anyway? She never used to be so bossy and interfering. In fact, they'd had a terrific relationship while Andrea was alive. But the minute John found himself a widower, Janet had seemed to feel as if it was her job to take care of him. She'd acted—*still* acted—as if he were incapable of making his own decisions.

"I don't understand you," she said. "What is it about that woman? Is it sex? Is that what—"

John stood abruptly, slamming his hand down on his desk. "Dammit, Janet! That's enough!"

"I-I'm sorry," Janet said, eyes wide as she backed away. "I didn't mean—"

"I know damn well what you meant," John said through gritted teeth. "Get this through your head. I don't have to explain to you or to anyone else why, when or how much I'm seeing Sydney. It's nobody's business but mine." He glared at his sister, his anger like an erupting volcano, impossible to stop now that it had started. "You know what your problem is? You need a few kids to worry about. Then you wouldn't have time to try to run my life."

Janet bit her bottom lip, and her hazel eyes filled with tears. "John..." She swallowed, her throat working. "I didn't mean . . . I only meant . . ."

"Oh, God," he said, bowing his head in frustration. He felt like a heel, especially after that crack about her needing kids. She and Mike had been trying to have kids for years. It was the big disappointment in their lives that they'd had no success. John ran his hands through his hair. "Look, I'm sorry. I shouldn't have said that. But you crossed the line and—"

"I know," she said, and he could see how hard she was trying not to cry. "You're right. It's none of my business. I just, well, I just *care* about you, and I hate to see you getting so involved with someone like her."

"Jan..."

"I know I'm the one who kept telling you to go out more, to start to date again," Janet persisted, her eyes beseeching him to understand. "But not with someone like her. You need someone who wants to be a stay-at-home wife and mother, who will be a help to you and the children."

"Look, I don't want to argue with you. I think it's best if we drop the subject, otherwise we're both going to say things we'll be sorry for later." John sat down again and turned his face toward the TV set. He ignored his sister.

A few seconds later, he heard her leave. When the door shut behind her, he sat there staring at the screen, but he was no longer listening or seeing anything except a replay of his argument with Janet.

He sat there for a long time. Long after *Geneva* was over. He only stirred when Emily knocked on the door and said, "Daddy, aren't you coming upstairs?"

He looked at the clock. It was five-thirty. "I'll be up in a few minutes, honey. Did you finish your homework?"

"Yes. I've been finished for *hours*." Emily always sounded like a prim little schoolteacher with her precise diction.

"What about your brother? Is he finished?"

Emily shrugged. "I guess so. He said he was done."

After she left, John shut off the TV. He closed the ledger he'd been working in before the *Geneva* show started. He felt depressed. He wondered if his depres-

sion was entirely due to his anger over Janet's interference.

Or could it just possibly have something to do with
the fact that Janet had only said the things he'd been
thinking all along?

Maybe he *should* break it off with Sydney. Wouldn't
it be easier on everyone if they called it quits now, before things got too complicated, before they began to
care too much?

Yet the thought of the lonely existence he'd led before Sydney had come into his life was intolerable. He
couldn't go back to that.

He just couldn't give her up.

Not yet.

Because Sydney had a college friend living in the
Chicago area, she stayed over after the taping on
Tuesday and spent the evening and following morning with Ann. On Wednesday afternoon, Ann took
her to the airport and Sydney boarded a plane to
Houston. The two-hour flight gave her a lot of time to
think. About John, and about her life and where it
was going.

Although she hated to admit it, her father was
probably right. The Montgomery case was going to
cause changes in her life. If that meant she would get
bigger and more challenging cases, she would welcome those changes. Sydney thrived on challenge, at
least as far as her work was concerned.

But if the changes meant more hoopla with the press
and being in the limelight all the time, she wasn't sure
she would be able to stand it.

Just look at this past week. She had gotten little or no concrete work accomplished because of all the phone calls and requests for interviews, not to mention the time it took to prepare for her appearance on *Geneva*.

It was her work she cared about. The issues. The people involved in the cases. Not the media attention.

In fact, if Sydney had her way, she'd never face a TV camera or newspaper reporter again. She knew she was probably in the minority as far as most ambitious lawyers were concerned, but that kind of attention was meaningless to her.

She sighed. She wondered if John had watched the show. Because of her flight, she would miss it, but she'd set her VCR to record it, and she would probably watch it tonight. See whether or not she'd come off the way she'd hoped to.

She had a feeling John had disapproved of her appearance on the show. She wondered why. A disturbing thought had occurred to her the other night, and she'd tried to shove it aside, but now it surfaced again. Could he be envious of her? And if he was, why? Hadn't he emphasized how much he eschewed the high stress and demanding aspects of his former career?

What am I doing with him? As she stared out at the pillowy clouds below, the question echoed in her mind. *I'm going to get hurt. I can tell myself a thousand times that I can handle anything that comes along, that I'm only in this relationship for the pleasure it gives me now, that I can walk away from him without regrets, but I no longer know if that's true.*

What was going to happen to her when John finally realized that the two of them were on different tracks? That her goals were incompatible with his?

How was she going to handle it when he dumped her?

She closed her eyes. There was no answer to the last question that didn't make her feel sick inside.

Because the unthinkable had happened.

She had fallen in love with him.

The next week flew by, and before Sydney knew it, it was the weekend before Thanksgiving. John took her to see *Madame Butterfly* that Saturday night. As they exited the Wortham Theater along with the other opera-goers, Sydney looked up to admire the Christmas lights on the sides of the downtown skyscrapers.

"That's my building," she said. "See? The one with the Christmas tree on the side."

John groaned. "Don't mention Christmas."

Sydney gave him a sympathetic look. "What's the matter? Haven't you done any of your shopping yet?"

"You mean you *have?*" he said incredulously.

She laughed. "No."

He laughed, too. "Thank God. I can't stand people who do all their shopping by October." He tucked her arm in his, and they walked toward where he'd parked his car. "I guess I'll go out this weekend and at least try to get the kids' stuff."

Sydney made a face. "Shop on Thanksgiving weekend? The crowds are horrendous."

"I know, but the kids are going to be away, so it'll be the best chance I've got."

"Where are they going?"

"To their grandparents' house." He looked at her. "Andrea's parents live in Florida. We, uh, have always spent Thanksgiving with them."

"But you're not going this year?"

"No."

"Why not?"

He hesitated a fraction of a second. "I didn't feel like it this year."

Something about the way he answered made Sydney's heart skip a beat. He hadn't *said* "because of you," but he'd implied it, she was sure. Happiness flooded her. She knew he was still close to his wife's parents, and that didn't bother her, not really. In fact, his generous, caring nature was one of the things she liked best about him. So how could she resent his continued affection for his children's grandparents?

"I guess you'll be spending Thanksgiving Day with your sister," she said after a moment.

"Nope. Janet and Mike are going to Massachusetts to spend the holidays with his family."

"Then you'll be here by yourself?"

"Looks like it."

By now they'd reached his car, and he unlocked the passenger door, then helped Sydney up into the Bronco. By the time he came around to his side and let himself in, Sydney had made a decision.

"John," she said as he pulled out of his parking slot on McKinney and headed toward Louisiana and the entrance to the Katy Freeway, "I'd like you to have Thanksgiving dinner with me . . . and my family."

She knew it was probably foolish and self-indulgent to have invited him, but she just couldn't resist showing him off. Couldn't resist showing her sisters and her mother that she could attract a man like John. That she wasn't a total dud in the romance department.

"I'd like that," he said.

Sydney smiled happily, trying to suppress her doubts. Part of her knew she would probably pay for this impulsive act. When she and John parted ways, she would have to put up with innumerable questions from her family if she led them to believe this was a serious relationship. And they *would* believe it was serious, because Sydney had never before brought a man home for them to meet.

It is serious. You're in love with him.

Sydney pushed the thought away. One of these days, she would have to deal with it.

But not today.

Thanksgiving Day turned out to be one of those perfect autumn days that Houston should have, but often didn't. It was clear, crisp, and just a bit chilly, with very little wind and no clouds to mar the surface of the robin's-egg-blue sky.

The sun danced off the patio doors—dazzling in its brilliance—and because they'd had quite a bit of rain for the past couple of weeks, the evergreens and fall gardens looked colorful and healthy. In a burst of domesticity the previous week, Sydney had bought two tubs of miniature mums, and their scarlet and rose blooms lent a touch of inviting color to her patio.

Sydney had called her mother a few days earlier to tell her to expect John for Thanksgiving dinner. Although her mother did a good job of acting as if Sydney's bringing a man to dinner was a common occurrence, Sydney knew that Helena was stunned.

John arrived to pick Sydney up at one, looking so handsome she almost forgot to breathe. He often had this effect on her, and she wondered if other women felt the same way when they saw the man they loved. He wore casual khaki pants and a cinnamon-colored cashmere sweater. She thought they looked good together, her teal pants outfit a nice contrast to his earth tones, then she had to bite her bottom lip to keep from laughing at herself. Since when had she cared about clothes and colors?

They got to her parents' home about one-thirty. Sydney had thought she might be nervous, but she wasn't. In fact, she couldn't wait to see the expressions on the faces of Wendy and Eliza.

Claire, of course, had already met John that last day in court. Sydney wondered if her sister had mentioned him to the others. Sydney had no idea how often her sisters talked to one another. She only knew that if they *did* talk, she was not in the loop. Even Claire, the sibling to whom she felt closest, never called her just to chat.

You don't call her, either.

As she and John exited his Bronco and walked up the driveway, Sydney decided she would try really hard today to get along with everyone and to avoid all negative thoughts. She would even be nice to Wendy's husband, Craig.

Her sisters didn't disappoint Sydney. Both Wendy and Eliza acted satisfyingly stunned when she introduced them to John. At first, their reactions gratified Sydney, but about midway through dinner, a creeping resentment began to eat away at her well-being.

During dinner, Eliza was seated directly across the table from John, and she'd been batting her eyelashes at him and giving him her one-hundred-watt smile from the moment she sat down.

"John, I think it's just *fascinatin'* that you gave up your law practice to be at home for your children," Eliza gushed.

At first, Sydney had been amused by Eliza's Southern belle act, but after a steady dose of it, Sydney wanted to vomit. She also wondered when and how Eliza had ferreted out that piece of information. Sydney hadn't heard John say anything about his reasons for going into the temporary employment business.

"It's too bad more men don't feel that way," Claire remarked before John had a chance to reply.

"How old are your children, John?" Wendy asked.

"My daughter just turned eleven and my son is six and a half."

"Oh, your daughter's only a little older than Caroline, then," Eliza said, inclining her head toward the kitchen, where all six of the grandchildren were sitting. "She's at the age where she's beginnin' to question everything I say. I'm really *dreadin'* the teenage years."

John smiled. "Yes, Emily already thinks she knows more than I do. I can't imagine what she'll be like in three or four years."

Eliza gave him a conspiratorial smile. "Has she started rolling her eyes at you yet?"

"Only about twenty times a day."

"Doesn't it make you *crazy?*"

John laughed.

"Sometimes I think there must be some kind of unwritten law. You know, *when a girl reaches the age of seven, she automatically knows everything.*" Eliza said.

"You should know," Claire said. "You were insufferable when you were little."

She still is insufferable, Sydney thought.

"I just thought girls were born thinking they know everything," John said.

Everyone laughed.

How did her sister do it? Sydney wondered. There wasn't a man alive who had ever gotten within ten feet of Eliza who Eliza hadn't managed to charm. She always found a subject near and dear to their hearts and then proceeded to monopolize the conversation. Sydney wished she could think of something to say, but when the subject was children, she had nothing to offer.

"Mom," Claire said, "the turkey is wonderful."

"Yes," the others chorused, offering various comments about the food.

"I like your dressing, Mrs. Wells," John said. "It reminds me of my grandmother's."

"Thank you, John."

Sydney felt absurdly grateful to Claire for changing the subject. The talk turned to more general topics, but Sydney noticed how Eliza continued to direct most of her remarks to John, and how much he obviously enjoyed her attention. He certainly made no effort to turn to Sydney very often.

In fact, he seemed to get along with all of her sisters extremely well. Too well.

Sydney wondered what was wrong with her that she felt so threatened by this.

Could it be the realization that any of her sisters, even Eliza, who Sydney considered vapid and stupid, was probably more suited to John than she was?

And if it had taken only a couple of hours in their company for Sydney to realize it, would it be very much longer before John himself realized it?

For the rest of the afternoon, Sydney couldn't shake the dismal thought. Even later, when everyone settled into the family room for coffee and dessert, and John sat next to her on the couch, casually draping his arm around her, Sydney didn't feel much better.

She looked at her mother and sisters and wondered why she had to be so different.

It had been a mistake to bring John here today.

Their entire relationship was a mistake.

Chapter Ten

"Sydney, I know something's bothering you," John said. He smoothed her hair back from her forehead and kissed her cheek. It was about midnight Thanksgiving night, and they were lying together in her bed after making love. "I wish you'd tell me what it is."

He felt her stiffen in his arms. He gently turned her face toward him and looked into her eyes. In the muted light, her eyes had the luster of dark pearls. "What is it?" he said.

She sighed, shaking her head almost imperceptibly. "Nothing."

"I don't believe you. Was it something that happened today?" It must have been, because on the way to her family's home, she'd been happy, even exuberant, if that adjective could ever be applied to someone as reserved as Sydney. But since they'd left her parents' place, she'd been remote. Even during their lovemaking, he had felt the distance between them.

When she didn't answer him, he said, "I really liked your family, by the way."

"That was certainly obvious."

John frowned. "What do you mean by that?"

"Oh, don't act as if you don't know what I'm talking about, John. God! I can't stand it when people play games." She turned her head away, and he could feel the tension vibrating through her body.

"Sydney," he said, totally bewildered. "I thought you'd be glad I liked your family." He gripped her chin and forced her to look at him. "What the hell is the problem here?"

For a long moment, she said nothing. Then, as if a dam had burst, she blurted out, "The problem is you hardly even knew I was alive today! You were so *fascinated* with Eliza and charmed by Claire and Wendy, you spent all your time talking to them. I might as well not have even been there."

John stared at her. So that was it. She was jealous! Sydney was jealous of his attentions to her sisters. He wanted to laugh, but he knew he'd better not. Sydney wouldn't take kindly to the idea that he thought her feelings were something to laugh about.

"Sydney," he said softly, smoothing his hand over her cheek. "Don't you know that the reason I paid so much attention to your sisters is that they *are* your sisters? Because you're important to me, and I wanted your family to like me?"

Her body still felt like a piece of wood in his arms. He sighed, letting go of her to reach over and turn on the bedside light so he could see her and she could see him. Sydney pulled the covers up and avoided his eyes.

He bent and kissed her neck. "There's absolutely no reason for you to be jealous."

Her head jerked around, and he received a painful bump on his nose.

"Jealous! That's ridiculous. I'm not the least bit jealous." She laughed, the sound cynical and bitter. "After all, I have no expectations from you. I know exactly what our relationship is all about. You don't need to sugarcoat it by pretending I'm important to you."

"And just what the hell is that remark supposed to mean?"

"You know exactly what it means," she said.

"If I did, I wouldn't ask you."

"Oh, come on, John, we're both adults. What's between us is great sex, nothing else." Her voice wobbled on the word *sex,* but she stuck her chin up in the air defiantly.

Her words cut him deeply, and he forgot to be cautious. "Oh, is that so? Then why'd you take me to meet your family?"

Her gaze met his, and there was a bleakness to it that caused his anger to evaporate as suddenly as it had formed. Her face had drained of color, and he could see she was struggling to pretend indifference.

He reached for her, and when he did he saw the sheen of tears in her eyes. He pulled her into his arms and cradled her against him, stroking her hair, even though she tried to push away. He lifted her chin and kissed her, deeply, trying to show her that he knew she didn't feel the way she'd pretended to feel, trying to show her how much she meant to him.

When the kiss ended, he held her face between his hands and looked deep into her eyes. "You mean a lot more to me than just someone to go to bed with," he said fiercely. "I love you. I love you, Sydney, and I think you love me, too."

"Oh, John..." A lone tear slipped from her eye and crept down her cheek.

"You do love me, don't you?" He brushed the tear away, an aching tenderness filling his heart.

"Yes," she whispered. "I do love you. I think I've always loved you." And then she cried in earnest. "I'm sorry I acted so stupid."

"Hush," he said, stroking her hair. "You weren't stupid."

Her voice was muffled against his chest. "Yes, I was. You're probably disgusted with me."

"I'm not disgusted with you."

She held him tightly. "I was so afraid you didn't love me. I tried to pretend I didn't care."

"I know." He'd done the same thing.

"John..." She looked up, her eyes brilliant, her eyelashes spiky and wet. "Say it again."

He smiled gently and kissed the tip of her nose. "I love you."

She sighed.

And then he kissed her and wondered what in Heaven's name he was going to do now.

* * *

Sydney knew if she lived to be one hundred, she would never have a Thanksgiving weekend as perfect as this one. Although she had intended to go the office on Friday, John wouldn't hear of it.

"You work too much," he said. "I want you to go shopping with me."

Sydney was thrilled. Not that she liked shopping that much, but the idea that John wanted her along made her feel good. She realized that even though he'd said he loved her, she still felt insecure about their future. She still wondered how she could fit into his life.

They went to Buffalo Bayou Mall, which was Sydney's favorite. She helped John pick out several books and games for both Emily and Jeffrey and watched as he tried to decide whether to buy them an expensive video game that he said they'd been wanting.

"Oh, what the hell. They'll only be kids once." With a rueful smile, he picked up the game. "I spoil them, don't I?"

Sydney just smiled. She remembered how her father used to lavish Christmas presents on her. Of course, they were never the kinds of presents her sisters received, but Sydney had always told herself she was glad. She was special. She didn't want dumb girl-presents like dolls and tea sets and jewelry.

Now she wondered what it might have been like if she *had* been treated like her sisters. Maybe she wouldn't have had so many stupid insecurities. And maybe she and her sisters would be better friends today. She shook off the memory. This day belonged to John. She didn't want anything to spoil it.

They ate lunch at the food court—Sydney laughing as John tried to get his mouth around an enormous gyro. She opted for pizza, which was easier to eat.

After lunch, they started looking for gifts for the rest of John's family. Sydney decided she might as well get things for her family, too. She was ashamed to admit it to John, but she usually took the easy way out and gave everybody except her parents gift certificates. She smiled, thinking how surprised they would be to see that she'd actually taken the time to shop.

She selected expensive cologne for Wendy, knowing that her youngest sister didn't have a lot of discretionary income right now. For Eliza, she decided on a designer scarf, and for Claire a leather handbag like the one John bought his sister.

They made several trips to the car to dump their packages in the trunk. At four o'clock, John said, "I'm ready to call it a day."

"Me, too," Sydney said thankfully. Her feet hurt.

"Do you mind if we go by my house? I'll drop this stuff off and check messages. I also told the kids I'd call today," John said.

"I don't mind at all."

As they were walking out of the mall, John suddenly stopped.

"What?" Sydney said.

John walked over to the window of a small boutique called Phoebe's. In the window was a winter scene, complete with Santa Claus and a sleigh. Sitting atop the sleigh was a blond mannequin dressed in a long-sleeved, full-skirted red wool dress with a low-scooped neckline trimmed in pearls and iridescent sequins.

"C'mon. Let's go in," John said. He grabbed her hand.

Sydney smothered her moan. She didn't feel like doing any more shopping. "Who'd you forget?"

He smiled. "I didn't forget anyone. I just saw something I want."

When they were inside, an elegant gray-haired saleswoman approached them. Her name tag said "Phoebe." She smiled. "Is there something I can help you with?"

"Yes," John said. "That red dress in the window. Do you have it in her size?" He gestured toward Sydney.

Sydney's mouth dropped open.

The saleswoman looked at Sydney critically. "Size ten?" she said.

"John," Sydney said, "I don't think—"

"I do."

"But, John—"

"Please, Sydney. Humor me, okay?"

Ten minutes later, Sydney stood in the dressing room and told herself not to be silly. Her admonition didn't help. She felt ridiculous, like a kid playing dress-up, or something. She didn't want to walk out and let John or the saleswoman see her in the dress. She knew she looked stupid. All she'd had to do was look at herself in the mirror. She simply wasn't cut out to wear a dress like this. She tugged the neckline up.

There was a discreet tap on the door, followed by, "Do you need some help?" from the saleswoman.

"Uh, no, I'm fine," Sydney said. She took a deep breath. Oh, well. She might as well get it over with. She opened the door and stepped outside.

John's gaze swept over her.

Sydney smoothed the dress down self-consciously.

"Walk over here," he said, and the look in his eyes made Sydney feel exactly the way she did when he touched her. She walked slowly toward him.

"Now turn around," he said softly.

She pirouetted slowly. When she was again facing him, she almost shivered at the way he was looking at her.

"It's perfect," he said, smiling.

"John, I don't think—"

"Don't you think it's perfect?" he asked the saleswoman.

"Oh, absolutely," she agreed.

Well, of course *she'd* agree, Sydney thought. Phoebe wanted to make the sale. One look at the price tag had told Sydney that. She started to protest again, but John ignored her.

"We'll take it," he said, handing his credit card to the saleswoman.

"Excellent choice. Now what about jewelry to go with it. I have some special earrings—"

"I don't need earrings," Sydney said. She drew the line at earrings.

"Let's not push our luck," John said, laughing, and the saleswoman gave a flirty little laugh in return.

Sydney frowned and returned to the dressing room. She looked at herself in the three-way mirror again. She thought about the expression in John's eyes. And for some reason, she was again reminded of all the Christmases when her sisters had gotten piles of frilly, feminine clothes and she'd gotten golf clubs and hunting rifles. She smoothed her hands over her rib cage and hips.

Then she smiled and carefully removed the dress.

They finally left the mall and drove to John's house. After he'd unloaded all of his purchases, checked his messages and called his children, he suggested they eat there. "I'll cook you dinner."

"Oh, John, it's too much trouble. You weren't planning to feed me. Let's just go out," Sydney said.

"It's no trouble. I like to cook."

Sydney marveled when she saw his freezer. He took out frozen asparagus and chicken breasts and a loaf of French bread. Sydney sat on a high stool and watched as he prepared the food. He was obviously one of those people who never measured anything. He chopped and trimmed and seasoned, all with a casual confidence that amazed Sydney.

About an hour after he'd started, they sat down to dinner. Besides the chicken, which he'd made with a mushroom-wine sauce, and asparagus, there was a saffron-flavored rice and the crusty bread, and John had opened a chilled bottle of a delicious Reisling to go along with their meal.

Sydney thought that even if she'd planned for a week, she wouldn't have been able to cook anything that tasted half as good. He was beginning to make her feel just as inadequate as her sisters did.

Why was it other people seemed to have so many talents, and she had so few?

As they neared the end of their meal, Sydney wondered if he'd want to spend the night at his house. She didn't think she wanted to. There were too many reminders of Andrea here.

He didn't suggest it, so they went back to Sydney's, and she was glad.

On Saturday, John suggested they go to the Arboretum to walk. "You don't get enough fresh air and exercise," he said.

Sydney thought how if anyone else had said that to her, she would have taken it as a criticism. With John, though, she didn't mind. She knew he was right.

After their long walk, John took her to Pappadeaux's for lunch, where they stuffed themselves on crawfish. During the afternoon, they went to a movie, something Sydney hadn't done in years. In fact, she couldn't remember the last time she'd spent a Saturday at the movies. She felt lazy and decadent.

They ate popcorn and held hands.

It was wonderful.

That night, John built a fire in Sydney's fireplace, and they spent the evening snuggled together on the couch. Later, they spread a quilt on the floor and made love in front of the fire. Still later, they sent out for a pizza.

"I can't believe I'm hungry again," Sydney said as she helped herself to her third piece.

"Sex makes you hungry," John said.

"Is that the collective 'you' or me in particular?"

He grinned. "I'm not sure. Do you want to help me conduct more research on the subject?"

On Sunday they slept late, then went out for brunch. Afterward, John asked Sydney if she wanted to go with him to pick up the kids at the airport. "I think it's time you get to know them," he said.

Pleasure mixed with uneasiness welled up in Sydney's chest. She knew she was good with kids. Even her sisters' kids seemed to like her a lot, but maybe John's children wouldn't. Maybe they wouldn't like it that she and John were seeing each other.

And what would John do if they resented her? Sydney had no illusions about John's priorities. He'd told her often enough that his children came first with him.

Riddled by doubts and feeling more insecure by the moment, she rode out to the airport with him. As they waited at the gate, she almost laughed at herself. Here she was, a woman who could face an entire courtroom with confidence, and now the prospect of facing two small children had her tied up in knots.

The deplaning passengers began filtering through the jetway.

"Here they come," John said. He grinned as first Jeffrey, then Emily, popped into view.

"Dad!" Jeffrey shouted, running the last few yards, then launching himself at John.

"Whoa," John said, but he laughed and lifted Jeffrey for a quick hug.

A more sedate Emily approached at a slower pace. She eyed Sydney curiously, then turned to smile at her father, who gathered her into his arms.

"I want you to meet a friend of mine," John said after they'd hugged. He smiled at Sydney. "This is Sydney. Sydney, Emily and Jeffrey."

"Hi," Jeffrey said, his green eyes friendly.

"Sydney's kind of a funny name, isn't it?" Emily said, her hazel eyes more assessing.

"Emily!" John said.

"Well, it *is*," Emily said.

Sydney smiled. "You're right, Emily. I've always wished I had a different name."

"Yeah, me, too," Jeffrey said.

Emily rolled her eyes. "Oh, Jeffrey, you do not."

"Do, too!" He stuck his tongue out at his sister.

"Do not." Emily gave Sydney a look of exasperation, and Sydney bit back a grin.

"Let's go get your suitcases," John said. His gaze met Sydney's over the heads of the children, who were still saying, "Do, too," and "Do not," and racing ahead of them. Now she did grin, and after a second, he grinned back.

Sydney felt as if she'd just passed her first test.

Chapter Eleven

The month between Thanksgiving and Christmas was one of the busiest months John's agency had ever had. John and his sister worked long hours, which was a mixed blessing for Sydney. She didn't get to see him as often as she would have liked, yet his heavy workload and his responsibilities as a father gave her much-needed catch-up time at work.

She'd neglected her work terribly since meeting John, and she knew she couldn't continue to do so. The end of the year was always a busy time for her firm, anyway, and this year was no exception.

Even though she would have liked to spend more time with John, the time she *did* spend with him was some of the happiest in her life. Sometimes she wondered if this was because John made each outing so special or if it was simply the fact that Sydney loved being with him, no matter what they were doing.

One Saturday, he made good on his earlier promise and invited her to accompany him and his children to the zoo. The day turned out to be wonderful. She wasn't sure what thrilled her more—the growing feeling of closeness with John or the easy camaraderie between her and his children.

She also had more fun than she'd have ever imagined possible. It was amazing to her that eating hot dogs and watching the antics of monkeys could be so exciting and special, but it was.

When the day ended, she knew she would remember it forever.

Another Saturday afternoon, they went to the Galleria, and all four of them skated at the indoor ice skating rink. Sydney only fell once, which she considered pretty remarkable considering she hadn't been on ice skates since she was twelve.

Emily and Jeffrey whizzed around the rink like old pros, and Sydney could see that they had skated often.

"Andrea was a pretty good skater," John admitted when Sydney asked him about the children's prowess. "In fact, when she was younger, she skated competitively."

Sydney noticed that John's eyes no longer got that bleak look when he mentioned his wife's name, and his matter-of-fact answer pleased her even as she wondered if she would ever be able to measure up to the multitalented Andrea.

But then John took her hand and said, "Come on, let's go. You've rested long enough," and they were off and onto the ice and laughing, and soon Sydney forgot all about her insecurities and Andrea's accomplishments.

After skating, they ate at a Chinese restaurant inside the mall, and Sydney marveled at how sophisticated his children were when it came to ordering.

"We took them out to eat as soon as they could sit in a high chair," John explained. A funny kind of expression slid across his face. "Neither one of us had much time to cook."

That was the first time he had ever uttered a word that could be construed as a criticism of his dead wife, and Sydney would have liked to question him further, but the presence of the children stopped her.

The following Sunday, Sydney and John took the children to see *The Nutcracker*, and although Jeffrey fidgeted through the performance, Emily loved the ballet, and so did Sydney.

Afterward, Emily said, "When I grow up, I'm going to be a ballet dancer." She pirouetted on the sidewalk in front of them.

"I thought you were going to be an astronaut," John said.

"I changed my mind," Emily said. "It's a woman's *pergative* to change her mind. Miss Traylor said so."

"I think the word is *prerogative*," John said. He grinned at Sydney over Emily's head.

Sydney bit her bottom lip to keep from laughing.

"You're dumb, Emily," Jeffrey pronounced. "Girls are dumb, aren't they, Dad?"

"I don't think I'll answer that, son," John said. He winked at Sydney, and now Sydney *did* laugh.

She laughed a lot when she was with John and his children, and it felt good.

Another weekend, John invited Sydney to go to church with him and the children, and afterward they went to Sunday brunch at Brennan's.

"I *love* this place," Emily declared, preening as their waiter fussed over her.

"I don't," Jeffrey said, pulling at his tie. "Don't they have hamburgers?"

Sydney grinned.

John kicked her under the table. "Quit laughing," he warned.

Only one element kept that month from being perfect, and that was the difficulty of finding any private time together. With children the ages of Emily and Jeffrey, John always needed a sitter if he and Sydney were to be alone. This meant they rarely went out, preferring to spend their precious time alone at Sydney's condo.

Sydney knew John was as frustrated as she was by this problem. She also knew that sooner or later she and John were going to have to talk about their situation. Several times, she wanted to bring up the topic, but at the last minute, she always lost her nerve. It was John's place to introduce the subject, she felt, and since he didn't, she was reluctant to do so. Besides, what would she say?

Let's move in together?

She almost laughed at the thought. John would never, not in a million years, consider doing anything even remotely like that.

What then? she wondered. Would she have to be contented with the status quo?

Or...?

Her mind refused to go to the next step. Because the next step would either be to say goodbye to John permanently or to marry him.

She couldn't bear to think of saying goodbye, and John had certainly never indicated any interest in marrying her. And even if he wanted to, could it ever work?

Because there seemed to be no answer to their dilemma, Sydney tried to just enjoy the moment and not worry about the future. And when she did occasionally allow herself to think ahead, she always got depressed. Then she'd get mad at herself.

Why are you always wanting more? John loves you. He tells you so. Often.

That had to be enough for now.

John knew he couldn't coast along like this forever. All through the month between Thanksgiving and Christmas, he tried not to think about the future. Yet he knew he could not put it off indefinitely. Very soon he was going to have to decide what to do about Sydney.

He had never expected to fall in love with her.

Yet he had.

And she loved him, too.

But being with her a couple of times a week wasn't enough. He wanted more.

A lot more.

He wanted to have Sydney in his bed at night and wake up next to her in the morning. He wanted her to be there at the end of the day, every day. He was tired of trying to find a sitter so that he and Sydney could be alone.

He began to give the matter serious thought.

There had to be a solution.

Sydney was more excited about Christmas this year than she had been in a long time. She knew John was the reason. She had invited him and the children to have Christmas Day dinner with her and her family, and he had accepted. In turn, he had asked her to spend Christmas Eve with him and his family. She had also accepted, although she was nervous about it.

She knew Janet was an adversary. Sydney had briefly been in Janet's company several times since that first encounter in John's office. Janet was always polite, but there was no warmth in her eyes, no real effort to go beyond the surface pleasantries.

Sydney wondered what she could do to win Janet over. Of course, if this relationship with John was only temporary—as Sydney kept reminding herself—it didn't really matter what Janet thought of her.

Yet deep down, in a hidden corner of Sydney's heart, she couldn't banish a tiny spark of hope.

Maybe, just maybe, there was a chance for her and John to build something more permanent. She felt encouraged by the fact that he had included her in outings with his children and that she got along well with both of them.

In fact, both children had managed to worm their way into Sydney's heart. Jeffrey was so open and friendly, it was impossible not to become attached to him. And Emily. Sydney smiled. She couldn't help feeling a special kinship with Emily, because they were so much alike. Sydney saw so many of her own personality traits in the youngster. Emily was a little perfectionist, and she wasn't afraid to set lofty goals for herself. She faced the world head-on, with courage and determination. She was just the kind of daughter Sydney would have wanted if she'd had children of her own.

So Sydney hopefully prepared for Christmas Eve.

"I'll pick you up about six," John said.

"John," Sydney said, "I'm a grown woman. You don't need to pick me up. I'm perfectly capable of driving to your mother's house by myself."

"I know that, but it's Christmas Eve. I don't want you driving home alone late at night."

"But you'll have the children with you, and they'll be tired."

"Sydney," John said firmly, "stop arguing with me. I'm picking you up and that's that. Let me worry about the kids."

When Sydney hung up the phone, she smiled. Although she had told John he didn't have to worry about her, it was nice to know he did. It had been a long time since anyone had worried about her—since she was a teenager, in fact. John's concern gave her a warm feeling.

The warm feeling made her feel more tolerant of the goofing off going on in the office that morning. Christmas Eve day was always a total loss as far as work production was concerned, and in other years, this fact had annoyed Sydney. Today she felt just as disinclined toward work as anyone else. The firm was closing at noon, and at eleven-thirty, Sydney walked around and distributed her Christmas gifts.

Norma squealed with pleasure over her gift certificate. "I know just what I'm going to get with it," she said. "A new pair of boots. Thank you, Miss Wells."

"You're very welcome," Sydney said. "Have a wonderful holiday."

"You, too."

Sydney smiled. She intended to. She hurried home to get ready for John's arrival.

"You wore the red dress," John said.

Sydney's heart beat faster at the look in his eyes.

He smiled into her eyes. "You look beautiful," he murmured. He walked inside her condo and shut the door behind him.

Then he took her into his arms and kissed her. John's kisses always made her greedy for more, and this one was no exception. After a long moment, he finally released her, saying, "We'd better go before I forget myself."

Twenty minutes later, he pulled into the driveway of a sprawling red brick ranch house located in Afton Oaks—an older Houston neighborhood inside the Loop. The house was set back on a large lot with several huge trees and was decorated lavishly. Multicolored lights defined the pitched roof and were dotted throughout the bushes and trees. There was a Santa-in-his-sleigh-with-his-reindeer scene on the front lawn, lighted by floodlights, and Christmas candles in all the windows.

As they walked up the luminaria-lined front walk, Sydney saw a sign that proclaimed the house had won second place in the Christmas decorating contest. It looked as if John's mother was also a multitalented woman.

Sydney took a deep breath. She tried to quell her nervousness and wondered if John's mother would react the same way toward her as John's sister had. God, she hoped not, or she was in for a long evening.

Without knocking, John opened the front door, and they walked into a small foyer. The scent of bayberry and pine greeted her, and she could hear muted laughter and voices coming from a room to their right. After helping her remove her coat, John—his hand settled firmly at her waist—drew her toward the room.

As they entered, Sydney briefly noted the enormous spruce tree in the far corner, the gaily wrapped packages piled under it and the pine boughs and ribbons festooning the mantel above the fireplace.

Janet and a pleasant-looking, sandy-haired man with blue eyes were seated on a chintz-covered love seat, and Emily and Jeffrey were sitting on the floor playing a game of Chinese checkers.

''Hi, Sydney,'' Emily said. She looked darling in a red velvet jumper and long-sleeved white blouse.

Jeffrey grinned. He wore a white pullover sweater and dark dress pants.

Sydney greeted the children, then turned to Janet, who looked festive and pretty in a dark blue velvet dress.

"This is my husband, Mike," Janet said. They both stood, and Janet smiled, but Sydney sensed a continued reserve and wondered if it would ever disappear.

Mike Cameron's blue eyes were friendly, though, and his smile seemed sincere as he welcomed her.

Just then, an older woman with salt-and-pepper hair and warm, dark eyes like John's, walked into the room. She wore an apron over her green wool dress and a big smile on her face.

"Sydney, this is my mother, Cecelia Appleton," John said. "Mother, this is Sydney. Sydney Wells."

"Hello, Mrs. Appleton," Sydney said, holding out her hand.

"Oh, please, my dear, call me Cecelia." John's mother grasped Sydney's hand in a firm shake. Her eyes were friendly as they appraised Sydney.

Cecelia Appleton looked a lot like her daughter, Sydney thought, but at least she seemed more open and receptive to the new woman in her son's life than Janet was. Sydney immediately felt more relaxed.

For the next thirty minutes, they sat and talked over glasses of wassail and nibbled at the cheese ball and crackers Cecelia Appleton had set out on a small cut-glass plate.

Then Cecelia excused herself. "I've got some last-minute things to do in the kitchen."

"I'll help you, Mom," Janet said, rising.

"No, you stay and visit," Cecelia said.

But Janet followed her mother out of the room, and Sydney was glad. Janet's presence made her feel too tense, too much as if she were on stage, and every word, every gesture, was being weighed and judged.

The reprieve only lasted fifteen minutes, then Janet reappeared in the doorway and said, "Dinner's ready."

The dining room was just as festive as the living room, with garlands of pinecones and silver ribbon adorning the buffet, a beautiful old mahogany table laid with a lace cloth and a centerpiece of red and white carnations and silver bells.

Sydney enjoyed the meal. John's mother and Janet's husband were both talkers, and kept the conversational ball rolling. Even Janet seemed friendlier.

Toward the end of the meal, Sydney said, "Cecelia, everything is delicious."

Cecelia smiled. "Thank you. I'll pass your compliments on to the chef."

When Sydney frowned in confusion, everyone laughed.

"My mother doesn't cook much," John explained.

"Got the whole thing from a catering service," Cecelia said, not the least bit apologetic.

Sydney decided she liked John's mother a lot.

After dinner, Sydney helped with the cleanup. As the three women worked in the kitchen, Cecelia said, "This is the happiest I've seen John in a long time." She gave Sydney a thoughtful look. "It's due to you, I'm sure."

Sydney felt a rush of warmth toward John's mother. "What a nice thing to say. Thank you." She wanted to look at Janet but didn't.

A few minutes later, Janet said, "I saw you on the *Geneva* show. You did a good job."

"Thanks."

"Geneva?" Cecelia said. "Really? You were on her show?"

"Yes," Sydney said. She explained about the Montgomery case.

"That was you?" John's mother said. "I read about it, but I never connected the name. Of course, John didn't tell me about you until only recently." She wiped off the countertop around the sink, then dried her hands in her apron. She turned and smiled at Sydney. "You must be very good."

Sydney shrugged. She hung her dish towel on the rack and removed the apron John's mother had insisted she wear. "I care about what I do."

"John used to be the same way," Cecelia said. "Sometimes I wish—" She broke off. "I talk too much."

"John is very happy doing what he's doing now," Janet said.

Sydney wondered what was going on.

After the cleanup, the three women went back to the living room, where the family exchanged presents. After asking John for ideas, Sydney had brought his mother a bottle of Kahlua as a hostess gift, but she hadn't expected to receive presents from John's family and was taken aback when Cecelia handed her a gift to open.

Inside was a hand-painted wooden box suitable for something small like paper clips or earrings.

"I made it myself," Cecelia said.

Sydney wasn't sure if she should be pleased at the thoughtfulness of the gift or unhappy because here was another woman in John's life who seemed able to do everything. Well, maybe not everything. Cecelia had admitted to not being able to cook.

Then John took a small box from under the tree and handed it to Sydney.

"But I didn't bring my present for you," Sydney protested. "I thought we were going to exchange gifts tomorrow."

"This is just a small gift. I've saved the other one."

There was an expression in his eyes that caused a flutter in her stomach, although she wasn't sure why.

When Sydney opened the box, she found a beautiful antique brooch inlaid with mother-of-pearl. "Oh, John, thank you. It's lovely. It'll look perfect on a suit lapel."

"That's what I thought."

After the gift opening, they listened to Christmas carols and drank coffee. Then, at about nine-thirty, John said, "Okay, kids. Time to get going. Remember, Santa is coming tonight."

Emily rolled her eyes, and Sydney repressed a smile. She knew the Santa talk was for Jeffrey's benefit. Earlier, John had explained that his mother was coming to his house to spend the night so that he could take Sydney home and not worry about the children.

After saying goodbye to Janet and Mike, Sydney and the kids piled into John's car, and Cecelia followed in her car.

"Come in for a minute while I get the kids settled," John said when they reached his house.

Twenty minutes later, they were on their way to Sydney's.

When they arrived, John built a fire in her fireplace while Sydney poured them each a glass of wine.

"Finally," John said as they sat close together on the couch. "I didn't think we'd ever be alone." He took the glass of wine out of her hands and placed it on the coffee table. Then he gathered her close, and they kissed.

When they finally drew apart, John stroked her cheek and looked into her eyes. "Merry Christmas," he said.

"Merry Christmas."

He kissed her again, this time with a tenderness that stirred her more deeply than she could ever have thought possible.

Then, still holding her close, he reached into his jacket pocket. "This is my other present," he said.

Sydney's hands shook as she accepted the small velvet jeweler's box.

He smiled. "Go on, open it."

Heart pounding, she snapped open the lid. Her breath caught. Inside, nestled into gray satin, was an emerald-cut diamond ring. Her thoughts tumbled wildly. What did this mean? Slowly, she raised her eyes to meet John's gaze.

"Will you marry me, Sydney?" he said. He removed the ring from the box and slipped it onto her finger. It glittered with a fiery brilliance.

Sydney swallowed. She opened her mouth to speak, but no words came out. Then suddenly, like the sun emerging from behind the clouds, her heart filled with an indescribable happiness. "Oh, John," she said, her voice breaking, "Yes. Yes, I'll marry you."

A long time later, John said, "I wish I didn't have to leave you tonight."

"I know." Sydney was lying in his arms, warm from the afterglow of their lovemaking and from the knowledge that one day soon, John wouldn't have to leave her and go home to a solitary bed.

"Let's get married soon," he said.

"How soon?"

He chuckled. "How about next week?"

Sydney knew he was teasing her, and even though she didn't want anything to intrude upon her happiness, she couldn't help but remember her full workload and the planning that was going to have to go into her taking time off to get married. For just a few seconds, she entertained the notion of suggesting they elope. She quickly discarded the idea. She knew John would want his children and family present, and she also knew her own family would be hurt if she were to exclude them. She sighed.

"What's wrong?" John asked.

"Oh, nothing. Just thinking how I don't know a thing about weddings."

"I'm sure your mother and sisters do."

Sydney didn't want to think about her mother and sisters. Her mother would probably want her to have a huge wedding with all her sisters as attendants. The thought gave Sydney a headache. "I need more time than a week," she finally said.

John smiled. "I know that. Well, how about a spring wedding? Will that give you enough time?"

"I'll make it be enough time," Sydney promised.

Sydney couldn't sleep that night. A couple of times she drifted off, but an hour later, she'd be wide-awake, hugging herself, so happy she thought she'd burst.

She still couldn't believe it.

Couldn't believe she was going to be John's wife.

Morning finally came, and with it bright sunshine, although when Sydney walked out onto her patio, she shivered. It was still cold.

When John arrived at noon, he brought the children up with him. They had decided last night they would tell them together.

"Do I have to call you Mom?" Emily asked after John broke the news.

Sydney smiled. "No, Emily, you don't have to call me Mom."

Jeffrey said, "Are you gonna live with us, Sydney?"

"Yes, she's going to live with us," John answered.

Later, as they drove to her parents' home, he said, "See? I told you they wouldn't mind."

Sydney glanced back at the kids. They were giggling together over some kind of hand-held game Jeffrey had gotten for Christmas. She wondered if her family would accept her news as matter-of-factly as John's children. "Did you tell your mother?" she asked.

He nodded.

"What did she say?"

"She was happy." He glanced at her. "She likes you."

Sydney smiled. "I like her, too." She hesitated. "What about Janet? Does she know?"

"Yes."

"And?"

He didn't say anything for a moment. Then he shrugged. "Jan will come around."

Sydney decided she'd never have a better opportunity to voice the question. "Why doesn't she like me, John?"

"She likes you."

He'd answered too fast, and Sydney wasn't fooled. "No. She doesn't."

He reached over and squeezed her knee. "I told you. She'll come around."

Sydney decided it didn't matter whether Janet came around or not. Sydney had lived with the disapproval of her own sisters all of her life. She guessed she could live with Janet's.

She smiled to herself. She could live with anything as long as she had John.

"Sydney!" Claire exclaimed. "Congratulations!"

As her mother and sisters crowded around her, looking at her ring and talking in excited voices, Sydney raised her eyes and met her father's gaze. It was his approval she wanted. After the initial excitement died down, he came over to her side and hugged her to him briefly. "Are you sure about this?" he said.

"Very sure."

But his question made her uneasy. Why had he asked her if she was sure? She watched her father carefully throughout the rest of the day. During dinner, she heard him questioning John about the agency.

"You able to make a good living with that agency of yours?" he asked.

Sydney cringed. If she'd been sitting closer, she would have said something to her father, but he wasn't looking at her, and she didn't want to shout across the table to get his attention. She hoped John wasn't offended. She tried to catch his attention, but he was already answering her father.

"The agency's doing all right. Not as good as we'd like it to, but it takes time to build a business."

Sydney sighed with relief. John didn't seem irritated by her father's personal question.

"Why'd you give up your law practice?" her father asked.

Where had her father been when her sisters were asking John the same questions at Thanksgiving? Sydney wondered. She couldn't hear John's answer because Eliza started talking to her. She resolved to talk to her father at the earliest opportunity.

The opportunity presented itself after dinner when Wendy's husband engaged John in conversation, and Sydney's father headed toward his study. Sydney knew her father wanted a cigar, but her mother had forbidden him to smoke one around the children.

She followed him. "Dad? Can we talk?"

"Of course."

Once inside the study, her father removed a cigar from the box on his desk. While he busied himself lighting it, Sydney plunged in. "Don't you like John, Dad?"

Her father looked at her squarely. "He seems like a fine young man."

"Why do I sense some reservation in that answer?"

He shrugged. "I *do* have reservations, but not because I don't like John."

"What are they?"

"One of them is what he does for a living."

"What's wrong with it?"

"What's wrong is that he's wasted doing what he's doing. I've talked to some people. The word is that John was a brilliant attorney, very respected, and he threw it all away to be some kind of Mr. Mom."

Sydney bristled at her father's derisive tone, even as she knew she'd had the same kinds of traitorous thoughts herself. "His children needed him. I admire him for putting them first."

Her father's blue gaze pinned her. "All right. Let's forget that for a minute. Let's talk about you, instead. How do you intend to manage a marriage, stepchildren, and your career?"

"Other women do," Sydney said.

"You aren't like other women."

"Gee, thanks for the vote of confidence." Sydney tried not to feel hurt, but she couldn't help it.

"You know what I mean. You're special, Sydney. You're going places. You're going to have to focus all of your energy on your career if you hope to realize your potential."

"You're saying I can't have a personal life?" Sydney said. "What about all the successful *men* out there who have big-time careers as well as a family life?"

Her father took a slow puff on his cigar before answering. "Those men have wives who support them by doing everything for them." He stared at her. "Will John support you that way?"

Her father's question disturbed Sydney a lot more than she wanted to admit. And as she returned to the living room to join the others, she knew she and John had to have a serious talk.

Chapter Twelve

"John, can I ask you something?"

John smiled lazily. Sydney sounded so pensive.
"Sure."

She traced a slow circle on his chest. "Are you
happy?"

His arm tightened around her. "Right now, I'd say
you'd have to look a long time to find a happier man
than me."

He slid his free hand down until it rested against her
bare hip. They had just made love, and he had the
luxury of not having to worry about getting right up
and hurrying home because the kids were spending the
night at his mother's. He was looking forward to the
time he never had to worry about leaving.

"I don't mean are you happy right this minute. I mean are you happy generally?"

John stroked her hip, thinking how good she felt. His hand crept around to cup her rounded bottom. He caressed it gently.

"John . . . stop that." She pushed his hand away. "Not now."

"Oh, you're no fun," he grumbled.

"Come on, John. Please be serious."

He gave an elaborate sigh, then sat up and snapped on the bedside light. "If you want me to be serious, I need light."

She sat up, too, bringing the covers with her. She propped her pillow behind her, then drew her legs up and rested her arms on them. She looked at him.

"Now what's this all about?" he asked.

"Just what I said. In general, are you happy with your life?"

"Of course I'm happy with my life. I've got the kids, and I've got you." He grinned at her. "What more do I need?" Playfully, he tugged at the covers.

She swatted at his hand. "That . . . isn't exactly what I meant."

"No? Well, what did you mean?"

"Are you happy with your job?"

John sighed. "Sydney . . . didn't we have this same discussion last week?" he said patiently, although he was beginning to be more than a little irritated. Just because he'd once mentioned that he sometimes missed his law practice didn't mean that he was unhappy. He wished he'd never told her that. Sydney reminded him of a wirehaired terrier they'd once had.

Give her something to sink her teeth into, and she never let go.

Sydney's eyes were troubled as they met his gaze. "Yes, but—"

"But what?"

"Well, my father and I were talking, and he happened to mention..." She hesitated as if suddenly unsure of herself.

John stiffened. "What did he *happen to mention* during this talk you had?"

"Only that it was a shame about your giving up your law practice. He said he'd been talking to some of your former associates and they all said how much your firm missed you and how much they'd like to have you back."

"I see. And just how did he happen to be talking to my former associates?" John asked, holding on to his temper by sheer force of will.

"I don't know," she said innocently. "Probably at a bar association meeting, or something. You know he's still active."

"And you, Sydney? Do you think it's a *shame* about my law practice, too?"

Her eyes were very blue as she met his gaze. "Yes, I do, because I think you miss it, just like your old firm misses you. I don't know why you're pretending to be satisfied with—"

"You know, Sydney," John said, cutting her off, "you might not mind your father orchestrating your life, but I sure as hell have no intention of letting him... or you... orchestrate mine. I think you're too obsessive about your work, that you should slow down—a lot—but have I said so? No. I've tried to respect your choices."

She stared at him.

"And I'll thank you to respect mine." He pushed back the covers and swung his legs out of bed. "End of discussion."

"John..." She reached for him.

He brushed her hands away. "It's late, Sydney. I've got to get going."

"John, please don't be mad. I didn't mean...I only thought..."

He turned to look at her. "I'm not mad."

"You *are* mad, and I only wanted—"

"I know exactly what you wanted. And I repeat, I'm not mad. I'm disappointed, though. I thought you understood where I'm coming from, but I can see I was mistaken." He left unsaid the thought that if he was mistaken about this, maybe he was mistaken about other things, too, but he knew she understood the implication. The understanding was there in the way she drew into herself, in the way her face was strained, in the way she tugged at her bottom lip— something he'd noticed her doing whenever she was nervous or uncertain.

He also saw the hurt in her eyes. But right now he didn't care. She had to learn that he wasn't one of her employees and she couldn't tell him what to do.

He stood and reached for his clothes. After he was dressed, he walked around to her side of the bed, leaned over and gave her a quick kiss. "Good night. I'll talk to you tomorrow."

"John..." She held out her hand.

After hesitating a second, he took it. It felt warm and smooth and strong as she wrapped her fingers around his.

"I love you," she said.

He nodded. "I know."

Thirty minutes later, as he pulled into his garage, he was still upset by their discussion. Was Sydney ashamed of him? Did she think what he did for a living was beneath her, or something?

And that damned father of hers! John had nothing against Sid Wells personally, but from everything Sydney had said over the weeks they'd been together, John had gotten a pretty good idea of the amount of influence Sid had had over his daughter's life. And now it looked as if her father thought he would be able to manipulate John the same way he'd manipulated Sydney.

It wasn't going to work.

John wasn't Sydney. He didn't care if the old man approved of him or not. John had good reasons for the choices he'd made, and those reasons hadn't changed. Wouldn't change. Because John had no intention of making the same mistakes he'd made before. Mistakes that had cost both him and his children.

For the first time in a long time, memories of the past crowded in on him. He remembered the intensity and excitement of his life with Andrea. The way they'd pushed each other, challenged each other. The way they'd packed each day to the fullest. Sometimes they'd only sleep three or four hours. Andrea used to say that sleep was such a waste of time.

"If I didn't have to sleep, I'd have so much more time to do everything I want to do," she'd exclaim.

John had only laughed. He'd enjoyed her drive and enthusiasm. He'd been the same way himself.

Yeah, and look where all of that intensity had gotten them. Andrea was dead. And his children were motherless.

No.

No way.

Never again.

He had learned his lesson.

He was perfectly happy with his life just the way it was. Going back to his old way of life would be the worst kind of betrayal.

His children needed him. He had built a safe haven for them, and he had no intention of abandoning it.

Not for Sydney.

Not for anyone.

But Sydney's questions had disturbed him, raising all his buried doubts about their impending marriage. Was he kidding himself that he and Sydney—two such different people with two such different paths in life— could possibly make a go of it?

The question refused to go away, and John had a hard time falling asleep once he finally got into his own bed.

Had he made a terrible mistake?

Again?

It took Sydney a week to get over feeling hurt by John's adamant refusal to even discuss his job situation. She told herself it was perfectly natural that he should be defensive. Perfectly understandable that he should lash out at her. Perfectly normal that he should view her concern as interference.

After all, a man's work was a touchy subject.

She hoped she hadn't jeopardized their relationship permanently by bringing up the subject of his job. Surely not. Surely John would get over his anger—for no matter what he'd said about not being angry with her, Sydney knew he was.

He hadn't even said he loved her when he left. She'd said, *I love you,* and all he'd said in return was, *I know.*

Oh, why hadn't she kept her mouth shut? Why hadn't she waited? It was probably too soon for her to have introduced the subject. What was her rush, anyway? Wouldn't she be in a better position to talk to him after they were married?

Once she had resolved this in her mind, she made a special effort to please John and not to overstep the boundaries he had erected. And gradually, as the weeks of January and February slid by, her efforts were rewarded, and Sydney felt their closeness returning. She breathed a sigh of relief. The crisis was past.

They began to talk about their wedding. Sydney thought April would be a good month, and John agreed.

Sydney's mother thought otherwise.

"I can't possibly make all the arrangements in two months, Sydney. The soonest we can get a wedding together is June."

"But, Mother, we don't want to wait that long," Sydney protested. "We just want a small wedding, anyway."

"Even so," her mother replied, "you have to find a dress, we have to hire a florist, book the church, find a place for the reception, order invitations, book a photographer. There are a hundred things to be done, and with your job, I doubt if you're going to have time to do any of them. That means I'll have to do them, and I need more than two months."

Sydney reluctantly agreed to a June wedding.

When she told John about her mother's proclamation, she expected him to object but all he said was, "Whatever makes you happy."

He tore a check out of his checkbook and inserted it in a waiting envelope. They were sitting in his office, talking while he paid bills.

Sydney took a sip of her coffee. "It's not what I want, but after she explained everything that's involved, I realized Mother was probably right. Plus, I hadn't even thought about this, but I've got to put my condo on the market, and we've got to find a place to live. That's all going to take time."

He looked up sharply. "Find a place to live?" He laid down his pen. "We have a place to live."

Sydney stared at him. She set her cup on the desk. "You mean here?"

"Yes. Where else?"

"You expect me to live here?"

"Of course, I expect you to live here. Why *wouldn't* we live here?" He frowned.

Sydney chose her words carefully. "John," she said gently, "try to understand. This is the house you and Andrea picked out. This is where the two of you lived together. I would never feel comfortable here. I'd always feel as if I were walking in her shoes."

He looked at her thoughtfully. "I can see how you might feel that way, but Sydney, I can't uproot the kids. This is their home. This is where all their memories are. I thought you understood that."

"Well, I do, but I guess I thought..." Her heart sank. Of course, John was right. Of course he was. It was foolish of her to feel so let down.

Later that night, as she brushed her teeth and prepared for bed, she kept telling herself that it would be okay. But she didn't believe it.

Would she be able to stand living in another woman's house? Wouldn't it be inevitable that John would make constant comparisons between Sydney and his dead wife?

Maybe the reason he didn't want to leave the house had nothing to do with his children. Maybe he wasn't ready or able to give up his own memories of the past.

Maybe he would never be able to forget.

Maybe Sydney was kidding herself that she'd ever be able to make him happy.

Maybe their engagement was a mistake.

Two weeks later, on a cold, bright February morning, Norma buzzed Sydney on the intercom. "Miss Wells, there's a Mr. Creighton on line one."

"Mr. Creighton? You mean, Neil Creighton?"

"Yes. With the Children's Advocacy League."

Intrigued, Sydney picked up the phone. "This is Sydney Wells."

"Miss Wells, hello. Neil Creighton, with the Children's Advocacy League."

"Yes, Mr. Creighton, I know."

"I've been hearing a lot about you lately," he said.

Sydney smiled. "And I've heard a lot about you for a long time." She waited, wondering if the league was going to refer a case. That would be nice.

"It's my pleasure to tell you that the board of directors of the league has voted to give you a special commendation for the work you've done on behalf of children's rights."

A glow of pleasure warmed Sydney. "Why, thank you. I'm flattered."

"It's very well deserved. And it's only the fourth time in the entire history of the league that we've done this."

"I hardly know what to say."

"You don't have to say anything. All you have to do is come to Washington on the 22nd of March to accept the award. There'll be a special ceremony at the White House, and an invitation to stay for dinner with the president and his family."

Sydney was thrilled. Although she didn't expect anything more in return for her efforts than the satisfaction of knowing she'd helped the children she represented, it was certainly exciting to receive an honor of this kind. And wouldn't her father be ecstatic? "I'm almost speechless," she finally said. "Of course, I'll be honored to be there."

"And your husband is invited, too, of course," Mr. Creighton continued.

"I'm not married, but I am engaged. Can I bring my fiancé?"

"Your fiancé is more than welcome."

When Sydney hung up, she hugged the knowledge of the commendation and invitation to appear at the White House to herself for a moment. Then she picked up the phone and dialed her father's number.

"I always knew you'd do something important, baby," he said. "You're on your way now!"

For a change, his exuberance and extravagant predictions didn't annoy her or make her feel uncomfortable. Instead, she just smiled. He deserved this moment of victory. He'd been a loyal believer for a long time, and he loved her.

"I can't wait," he declared. "Think of it. The White House! I've never been to the White House."

Suddenly, Sydney realized he expected to go to Washington with her. "Dad..."

"Wait'll Francis Folger hears. You'll probably get a huge raise. And just wait'll *Craig* hears. He's always been jealous—"

"Dad! Will you listen for a minute?"

He finally stopped talking. "What?"

"I'm sorry, Dad, I know how much you'd like to be there, but, well, John will be going to Washington with me."

There was silence for a long moment. Then he said, "I guess I wasn't thinking. Of course, you'd want John to go."

After they hung up, Sydney sat there. Some of her happiness had been diluted by her father's obvious disappointment over not being able to see her get her commendation. She sighed. Well, it couldn't be helped. Although she'd love to make everyone happy, it wasn't possible, and right now, John was more important than her father. Her future with John was more important. Her father realized that.

Smiling again, she picked up the phone.

When John's intercom buzzed, he answered absently, "John Appleton." He was in the middle of payroll, which required all of his concentration.

"Hi. You busy?" It was Sydney.

"Never too busy to talk to you." Propping the phone on his shoulder, he made another entry, saved it, then turned away from the computer screen. "What's up?"

He listened as she told him about her phone call from the Children's Advocacy League. Myriad emotions played through his mind as she talked. Uppermost was pride in her. He knew this commendation was validation and recognition for her hard work and dedication.

"That's wonderful," he said when she'd finished. "You deserve it."

"I want you to go with me," she said.

"I'd love to go with you."

"My father was so excited when I told him."

Before he could stop himself, John said, "I should have known you'd call your father first." He was immediately sorry. His reaction was petty.

"Oh, John, I'm sorry. I didn't think—"

"Forget it. I'm the one who's sorry. I know how much this must mean to your father."

"I know it must seem as if I care more about him than I do about you, but it's just that all these years he's been so encouraging and supportive."

"I know. It's okay. You don't have to apologize."

They talked for a few more minutes, then hung up.

Off and on for the rest of the afternoon, John thought about their conversation. He was happy for Sydney, but he couldn't help wondering what ramifications this commendation would have on her life. On their future. He also couldn't help feeling just a tiny seed of envy. He knew the emotion wasn't worthy of him, and he tried to ignore it, but it sat there, at the back of his mind, like a splinter that is embedded deep in the skin and is impossible to dig out.

After dinner that night, he settled the kids in bed and made his nightly call to Sydney.

"Guess what?" she said excitedly. "Mr. Folger said the firm is going to have a big reception in my honor next Friday night."

"I thought you didn't like stuff like that," John teased. He was determined not to let Sydney know that he had even one negative feeling about the day's events.

"I usually don't, but, I don't know, this is really special to me, John. Do you think I'm being silly?"

"No. In your shoes, I'd feel the same way."

"Would you?"

He heard the uncertainty in her voice and knew she needed his wholehearted support. "Yes. And if I haven't told you before, I'm proud of you."

There was silence for a moment, then she said, her voice husky, "I love you."

"I know. I love you, too."

John stood beside Sydney the Friday of the reception and kept reminding himself of his good resolutions.

But it was hard.

Francis Folger approached him about midway through the reception. John knew Folger slightly. "Hello, Mr. Folger," he said as Folger walked up.

"Appleton," Mr. Folger said, "good to see you again. How are you doing?

"I'm doing well."

"I was sorry to hear you'd left Chasan & Jeglinski. Don't suppose you're in the market for a new job? We're always looking for good people."

John smiled. "Thanks, but I'm pretty happy with what I'm doing."

"Some kind of personnel agency, isn't it?"

"Yes. We specialize in legal temporaries. As a matter of fact, your firm uses us."

"Really? Well, you must be good."

"We are." John would have elaborated, but Folger's attention had obviously wandered. He had that look that people get when they are no longer interested in a subject but aren't quite sure how to escape.

His gaze lighted on Sydney, who stood a few feet away. He smiled. "We're very proud of Sydney," he said. "She's a real asset to the firm."

"Yes. I'm proud of her, too."

"She's accomplished what very few people are able to do," Folger continued. "Just think of it. A White House ceremony. Isn't that something?"

"Yes," John agreed.

"The prestige she's brought to our firm is worth a lot to us. And she's only begun. That's the beauty of it."

"Yes," John said again. He was beginning to wish he'd stayed home. He felt like a fifth wheel. Sydney didn't need him here. Hell, she'd hardly looked in his direction for at least half an hour.

Francis Folger walked away a few minutes later, and John headed for the bar. Once he had a fresh drink, he stood off to the side and watched Sydney across the room. She looked beautiful tonight. She'd bought a dark blue cocktail dress for the occasion. It was a short, off-the-shoulder number he'd helped her select, and it not only showed off her beautiful shoulders, but exposed a lot of her legs. He still couldn't believe she'd ever thought she was anything but beautiful.

He watched as well-wishers crowded around her. He saw how she smiled and laughed. Her face was flushed with excitement. Any man would be proud to call her his. John watched her, deep in thought, and didn't realize someone had joined him until he spoke.

"Kinda hard being engaged to old Sydney, isn't it?"

John turned. The man who had spoken was Doug Farrell, the jerk who had been so obnoxious to Sydney that first day when John worked as her paralegal.

"I don't find it hard at all," John replied coldly.

Farrell shrugged, but his eyes contained a sly expression. "I guess you must be one of those liberated guys who don't mind a woman wearing the pants in the family, huh?"

John stared at Doug. He considered several options, one of which was to aim a well-placed blow right in the middle of Farrell's smarmy face. "If I were in your shoes, I'd be jealous, too," he finally said. Then he walked away.

But Farrell's attitude bothered him, and John wondered if all the rest of Sydney's associates were thinking along the same lines.

For the rest of the evening, John had a hard time keeping a pleasant smile on his face. Everything anyone said to him seemed suspect, and he kept looking for hidden meanings.

Sydney, on the other hand, bubbled with excitement. When the reception was finally over, and they were on their way home, she talked a blue streak.

"Did you see old Mr. Hubbard tonight?" she said. "I couldn't believe he actually came to the reception. He never comes to anything anymore."

"Well, this was pretty special," John said. "It isn't everyday one of their employees is invited to the White House."

"Oh, John, I really *am* excited about this."

"I know you are."

When they arrived at her condo, he kissed her goodnight at her door.

"Aren't you coming in?" she said.

"I'd better not." He knew it was small-minded of him, but he just couldn't keep up the pretense of one-hundred percent enthusiasm. Maybe tomorrow, but he'd had enough of everything tonight.

"But it's early, and I thought..." Her voice dropped, and her eyes held an invitation. "I thought we'd celebrate."

He forced a smile. "I know. I wish I could, but the sitter can't stay late tonight."

"Well, okay..." Her face reflected her disappointment.

At that moment, John didn't like himself very much. Because he was feeling guilty, he gathered her close and held her for a moment.

"I really am sorry," he said.

She lifted her face. "I know. It's okay."

All the way home, he told himself that it wasn't Sydney's fault she had the kind of success he'd always envisioned for himself.

You'd better get used to it. Francis Folger was right tonight. This is only the beginning for Sydney. And you're going to have to learn how to live with it.

Chapter Thirteen

Sydney floated through the next few days. She'd never realized she was the sort of person who would get such a kick out of praise and recognition.

It was embarrassing to find out she wasn't as high-minded as she'd thought she was. That she enjoyed the awe she saw in the eyes of the younger associates, and the respect—some of it grudging, she was sure—from the more experienced members of the firm.

It gave her particular pleasure to see Doug Farrell's obvious envy. She didn't even mind that he tried to make light of her accomplishment. His pettiness hurt him a lot more than it hurt her.

But her euphoria was tempered by the knowledge that something was wrong with John. She hadn't seen him since the reception on Friday, and although they'd talked on the phone each evening since, he had seemed distant. On Monday evening, she finally decided to say something.

"John, what's wrong?"

"What do you mean?"

"I don't know. That's why I'm asking. But you just seem so preoccupied and distant. Did I do something?"

"No, of course not," he said. There was no hesitation at all in his answer. "I'm just worried about Emily."

"Emily?"

"She's been sick since Saturday morning."

"Why didn't you tell me?"

"I thought I did."

"Well, you didn't," Sydney said. She wanted to say more, but contented herself with, "What's the matter with her?"

"She's got a strep infection, and she's been running a fever. She'll have to stay home from school, probably all week."

"Knowing Emily, she's probably chomping at the bit."

"You could say that," John said.

Although John's explanation made perfect sense, something about it didn't ring true to Sydney. Certainly, he was concerned about Emily. But his distance from Sydney had begun before Emily got sick. It had started Friday night.

There was only one reason for his behavior that Sydney could see. She was afraid John was jealous of her success, even if he hadn't admitted his feelings to himself. And if that was true, what could she do about it? Not much, especially when he wouldn't even discuss his job situation, let alone admit he wasn't happy. If only he'd be honest with her.

She was mulling over this problem when, about three o'clock that Tuesday afternoon, Norma buzzed her to say Mr. Creighton was calling again.

Sydney picked up the phone eagerly. "Mr. Creighton! Hello!"

"Hello, Miss Wells."

"Can I ask you a favor?"

"Of course."

"Miss Wells sounds so formal. Do you think you could call me Sydney?"

He laughed. "That's easy enough. I'd be happy to, but only if you'll call me Neil."

"It's a deal." She smiled. "Neil."

For a few minutes, they talked about Sydney's upcoming trip to Washington.

Then Neil Creighton said, "But your trip isn't the only reason I called. There's something else I wanted to discuss with you, Sydney."

Sydney waited.

"Vicki Booker, who's been our lead counsel here at the league for the past twelve years, has given her notice. She'll be leaving us the first of May."

Sydney admired Vicki Booker's work. The woman was a brilliant litigator and a much-feared adversary in the courtroom. The league would have a hard time finding anyone even half as good to replace her.

"I'm sorry to hear that," she said. "She's been my role model for years."

"Yes, we're sorry, too. We'll all miss Vicki, but change is inevitable. No one stays forever."

"It's good you can be so philosophical about it."

"I have to be philosophical. There's nothing I can do to change things. Vicki's not leaving to take another job or anything like that. Her husband is ill, and she wants to be at home for a while."

"Even so, I'll bet it's going to be difficult to replace her."

"Well, actually, not so difficult." He chuckled. "Haven't you figured it out yet, Sydney? After a lengthy discussion, the board of directors has voted unanimously to authorize me to offer you the position of lead counsel."

Sydney had just picked up her water glass to take a sip, and she almost choked when Neal Creighton's words sank in. Her! They were offering *her* Vicki Booker's job. Her hand shook as she set her glass down.

"Are you all right?" Neil asked.

"Y-yes. I—I just choked on some water, that's all." Sydney coughed, then cleared her throat. "Mr. Creighton...uh...Neil, you took me completely by surprise. I had no idea that's what you were leading up to."

He chuckled again. "Well, now that you do, how do you feel about it?"

"I—I don't know. I'm...immensely flattered, of course, but..."

"I was afraid there might be a but," he said.

"The thing is, a few months ago I would have jumped at this chance. Now, though, things are a bit different. I just got engaged, and my fiancé owns a business here in Houston, so I've someone other than myself to consider. Could I have a few days to talk it over with him?''

''Well, of course...if you need some time, you must take it. Take as long as you need. Although we *would* like an answer as soon as possible, because if you're not going to accept, we'll have to find someone else. We'd like whoever will be replacing Vicki to come on board by the first of April or at the very latest, the fifteenth, so the new counsel can spend some time with Vicki before she leaves for good. Of course, she'll be available later on for questions and things like that, but it won't be the same as working with her on a daily basis.''

''I understand.'' Sydney's mind whirled. Delight, exhilaration, and then trepidation over John's reaction to this latest piece of news, all churned together to make her feel almost light-headed. ''I'll make my decision soon. I promise.''

She knew Neil Creighton had been surprised by her request for time. What he was offering her was a plum, one he had surely expected her to snatch without a second's hesitation.

But how could she have? She couldn't do something that had such far-reaching ramifications without talking to John. He was too important to her for her to jeopardize their relationship, no matter what the reason. She *had* to include him in the decision.

For the next few minutes, they discussed terms, then Neil said, ''I'll look forward to hearing from you. And Sydney?''

"Yes?"

"I do so hope you'll take the position. You'd be a wonderful successor to Vicki. A worthy successor."

"Thank you, Neil. Just having you offer me the position means a lot to me."

After they hung up, Sydney sat there in a state of stunned disbelief. Never had she imagined anything like this happening. It was wonderful. It was fabulous! She felt like dancing around the room, but contented herself with replaying the conversation in her mind.

Oh, God, she wanted the job so badly. She had wanted to shout *Yes, yes, I'll be there tomorrow if you say so!* when Neil Creighton had made his offer. It had taken all her self-control to ask for time to talk to John.

Some of her happiness faded as she thought about John. What would he say when she told him? Would he be happy for her? Would he finally be willing to change his life to allow her this opportunity?

Or would she have to decline? Oh, God, she couldn't turn this down. Surely she wouldn't have to. Surely this news would be the catalyst that would snap John out of his ennui. Surely now he would realize that he could no longer hide from real life. Surely he would urge her to accept and assure her that he would be there for her, every step of the way.

Yes, she told herself, of course, that's what would happen, because the alternative was unthinkable.

She couldn't say no to this offer. The thought of turning down the job made her feel almost sick inside. It was such a fantastic opportunity the Advocacy League was offering her. The opportunity of a lifetime. A pinnacle of success for someone in her field.

If she took the position of lead counsel for the league, she would no longer have to worry about billable hours, no longer have to put up with the politics of a firm like Folger & Hubbard, no longer have to bite her tongue and accept the kind of subtle discrimination dished out by some of her male co-workers.

She would live and work in Washington, D.C. She would be a part of something important, an organization that was doing work that would have long-range effects in her field. She would be a mover and shaker, just as her father had predicted long ago.

Her father!

He would pass out from excitement when he heard the news. How she wished she could call him and talk to him about this, but she knew that was impossible. John deserved to be the first person she told. She would talk to him tonight. She was supposed to go over to his house for dinner at seven-thirty, anyway.

For the rest of the afternoon, she couldn't concentrate on her work. All she could think about was the telephone call from Neil Creighton.

Finally, at five-thirty, she decided to call it a day. She wasn't accomplishing anything anyway, so she might as well go home. She began cleaning off her desk. Just as she'd finished putting some papers into her briefcase, her intercom buzzed, and the switchboard operator announced that her father was on line two.

"Sydney?" His voice vibrated with excitement. "Sydney, I just got a call from Senator Gavin." Clifford Gavin and Sydney's father had been law school roommates. "He told me he heard through the grapevine that you're going to be offered the job of lead counsel for the Children's Advocacy League."

Sydney grimaced. Damn. Why did her father's connections have to be so good? And so speedy with the news?

"Sydney? Did you hear me?"

"Yes, Dad. I heard you."

"Well? Is that *all* you have to say? Aren't you excited? By God, this is the kind of thing I *knew* would happen. Lead counsel for the Advocacy League! Sydney, nothing's going to stop you now. I told you your name would be a household word. I'm so proud of you, I could burst! I wonder when they'll call you?"

"I've already gotten the offer, Dad, but I, uh, I'm not sure I'm going to accept." Saying the words out loud gave her that sick feeling again.

"Not going to accept! What do you mean? Are you crazy? This is what we've worked for all these years! Of course, you're going to accept."

"*We've* worked for?" Sydney was unable to stem the tide of resentment that swept through her as she zeroed in on the phrase that had caused it.

"Oh, you know what I meant," her father sputtered. His voice dropped soothingly. "Aw, come on, baby, you were kidding your old man, weren't you? You wouldn't turn down an opportunity like this."

Sydney sighed, her resentment ebbing. How could she stay mad at her father? Especially when she wanted exactly what he wanted for her. "I don't want to, but I can't accept until I talk to John about it. If he's not willing to go to Washington, I-I don't see where I'll have any other choice."

There was silence for a long moment. Then her father said, "Promise me something, baby."

"What?"

"Promise me that no matter what John says, before you call the league with your answer, you'll talk to me first. Will you promise me that?"

Sydney decided his request was reasonable and the least she could do, especially if...no, she refused to think along those lines. John would never ask her to turn down the job. "Okay," she said. "I promise."

The office phone rang a few minutes after six. Janet had left early that afternoon, saying she and Mike had an appointment. John was already on his way upstairs, and he decided he'd just let the answering machine pick up. He didn't feel like talking to any more clients today. He was tired, and he needed to check on Emily.

But curiosity drew him to the machine.

"This is Sid Wells, John. It's urgent that I talk to you as soon as possible. Could you please call me?"

John grabbed the receiver before Sydney's father broke the connection. Fear engulfed him. Had something happened to Sydney? "Sid? I'm here. Is something wrong?"

"John, oh, good. Glad you're there. No, nothing's wrong. I just need to talk to you."

"Oh?"

"But I'd prefer to talk in person. Could you meet me for drinks somewhere?"

"No, Sid, I'm sorry. I can't. My daughter's sick, and I can't leave."

"How about if I come over there, then?"

"When? Now?"

"Yes, now."

"Will this take long? Sydney's coming over for dinner at seven-thirty."

"It won't take long. And since I sure don't want Sydney there when we talk, I guess I'd better hurry. I'll see you in twenty minutes."

Sid Wells was as good as his word. Twenty-five minutes later, glasses of scotch in hand, the two men were sitting in John's living room.

"I'll get right to the point," Sid said after taking a swallow of his drink.

"Good." John couldn't imagine what Sid Wells had to say, especially if he hadn't wanted to say it in front of Sydney.

"Sydney got a call from Neil Creighton today."

John frowned. "Neil Creighton?"

"You know. The director of the Children's Advocacy League."

"Oh, yeah . . ."

"He told her that the lead counsel for the league has resigned." Sid's gaze met John's. "He offered Sydney the job."

John's first reaction to Sid's news was anger. Why was it that any time something important happened with Sydney, she always talked to her father about it first?

After the anger came a sinking feeling of dread. Even though John had never worked in Sydney's field, he knew enough about it to know that a job offer like this one was something most people only dreamed about.

"You know what this means, don't you?" Sid said, eyes narrowed.

John fought to control his emotions. He had no intention of allowing Sid Wells to see how his news had affected him. "Of course I know what it means," he managed to say in an unemotional voice. "It's quite a coup for Sydney."

"You bet your boots, it is. Hell, it'd be quite a coup for *anyone,* not just Sydney!"

"I know that." What did Sid Wells think? That John was stupid?

"Oh, yes," Sid continued as if John hadn't spoken. "That job is a once-in-a-lifetime opportunity. It's the kind of thing Sydney has worked toward for years." He paused, giving John an intent look. "She'd be a fool to turn it down."

John nodded. A leaden unhappiness settled over him. "Yes, she would."

"Would it surprise you to find out she told me she *might* turn it down?" Sid continued, his blue gaze relentless as it pinned John. "She said her decision hinged on you and what you had to say."

At least she had considered John's feelings.

"I know you won't stand in her way, though," Sid said. "Because if she turns down this job, she'll regret it the rest of her life. You don't want that, do you?"

"No. Of course I don't." Sid was right. She would regret it. And that regret would color their entire relationship. Would eventually ruin their entire relationship.

"Then it's up to you to see that she doesn't turn it down," Sid said. He drained his glass. "I'd better be going. Think about what I said."

As if he could think about anything else, John thought after Sid left. He hated to admit that Sydney's father was right about this, but of course, he was.

Sydney loved her work, and she was exceptional at it. John had seen that for himself the day he'd worked for her. He'd seen it again when he'd watched her in court during the final arguments on the Montgomery case. And he'd heard it every time she discussed any of her cases.

This job would be the perfect showcase for her talents. It would give her the kinds of challenges and exposure most defense attorneys would give their eyeteeth for. It would test her abilities to the limit, and be invigorating and inspiring and rewarding.

If she turned down this offer from the Children's Advocacy League, not only would she regret the decision, she would also grow to resent John for forcing her to make it. Eventually, she would hate him.

His heart felt like a stone in his chest as he realized exactly what he must do.

Sydney had butterflies in her stomach as she pulled up in front of John's house. It was exactly seven-thirty. She took several deep breaths as she walked up the front walk and onto the porch.

Oh, John, please be happy for me. Please say it's okay.

She rang the doorbell. A few minutes later, John opened the door. He smiled at her.

"Hi," he said softly.

"Hi."

He drew her inside, then put his arms around her and held her close. "I've missed you," he said.

She wrapped her arms around him tightly. "Oh, John, I've missed you, too."

He kissed her then—a lingering kiss that stirred Sydney deeply. When the kiss ended and Sydney looked into John's eyes, she felt confused. He seemed so serious. Sad, even. She wondered why. She looked at him quizzically as he released her, but he avoided her gaze.

"Do you want to say hi to Emily before we have our dinner?" he said.

She smiled. "Yes, I do. I brought her something." She pointed to the shopping bag she'd set down when she first walked in.

"Let's go upstairs," he said.

Sydney followed John up, and he led the way to Emily's bedroom. Emily looked pretty good. She was sitting up in bed and watching television.

"Hi, Emily," Sydney said. "How are you feeling?"

"Okay. I wish I didn't have to stay in bed, though."

"I brought you something." Sydney handed Emily the package.

Emily tore off the wrapping paper. She grinned. "A book!" She looked at the cover. "*Song of the Buffalo Boy* by Sherry Garland," she read out loud. "Gee, thanks!"

"It's autographed," Sydney said.

"It is? Gosh, I've never had an autographed book before."

John leaned over the bed and kissed Emily's cheek. "Do you need anything, honey?"

"Some more orange juice," Emily said.

While John got Emily her juice, Sydney walked back to the playroom to find Jeffrey. He squealed with delight over the puzzle she'd brought for him.

By the time Sydney walked into the living room, John was already there. "I ordered Chinese food. Is that okay with you?" he said.

"Anything's okay with me," Sydney said.

"It'll be here in about fifteen minutes. Do you want a drink while we wait?"

She shook her head. "No, I, uh..." She sighed. "John, there's something I have to tell you." She might as well get it over with right away. Otherwise, she'd go crazy from nerves.

He listened quietly as she related her conversation with Neil Creighton. As she talked, she searched his face. What was he thinking? It was impossible to tell. "The offer is wonderful, isn't it, John?"

"Yes, it *is* wonderful. When do they want you to start?"

"The first of April, but I haven't said yes yet. I-I really want to take it, of course, but...I'll turn it down if you want me to,'' she said in a rush. "You're more important to me than any job, John. I want you to know that.''

He nodded, a funny little half smile on his face. "I'm really proud of you, Sydney. You know that, don't you?''

Sydney hadn't even known she was holding her breath until she expelled it. Relief flooded her. It was going to be all right.

"And I would never expect you to turn this job down,'' he continued. "For me or for anyone else. This is what you've worked for all these years. You've got to take it.''

"Oh, John,'' she exclaimed happily, "it's going to be so good for both of us. You'll see. You won't ever be sorry. And I just know you'll find a wonderful job in Washington, too.'' She beamed at him. "Maybe it was all meant to happen this way. For us to start our life together somewhere new.''

His dark gaze met hers, and the expression in his eyes caused her stomach muscles to clench in sudden uncertainty. "I can't go with you, Sydney.''

"You can't go with me?'' she repeated dully, refusing to believe what she was hearing.

"I'm very sorry. I wish I could, but it's impossible. My life is here.''

"Well, then I won't go eith—''

"Don't be stupid. Of course, you're going. This is the chance of a lifetime. I don't *want* you to turn the job down.''

"But, John," Sydney said, pain tearing through her. Didn't he love her? Didn't he want to marry her? Didn't he *care?* What was he saying?

"In your place, I'd take it," John said. He gave her that little half smile again. "And never look back."

Sydney's heart was beating too hard. She felt as if she might faint. Why was he doing this? How could he show such a callous disregard for what they had shared, for what they meant to each other? How could he so easily dismiss their plans and hopes for the future?

I'd take it and never look back.

The words battered her. They were the most wounding words she'd ever heard. How could he say them? Surely he didn't mean them!

Her pride almost caused her to walk away. But something, some hint of sadness in the back of his eyes, some flicker of pain that he was trying to disguise, stopped her. He didn't mean any of this. She was sure of it. She remembered what her father had always told her about going after what she wanted. He'd always said she was a fighter, that she never gave up.

"John, I don't know why you're doing this," she said reasonably. "Out of some misguided sense of pride, maybe. Or maybe you're just plain afraid, but you don't have to be. It'll all work out. We can be happy in Washington. In fact, it'll be good for—"

"Afraid!" His jaw hardened, and his dark eyes glinted with anger. But when he spoke again, his voice was mild. "Let it go, Sydney. Just let it go, okay? Before we both say things we'll regret later." He leaned forward, taking her hands in his. He rubbed the tops of them with his thumb. "Let's try to part as friends."

Suddenly, the doorbell rang, and John released her hands. "Our food is here."

While he went to answer the door, Sydney tried to repair her shattered emotions. She didn't know what to do. Nothing had turned out the way she'd imagined.

When John returned, he set the bag of food on top of the card table. "Shall we eat while it's hot?" he said.

"I can't believe you just expect me to eat as if nothing's happened," Sydney said. She walked over to him, sliding her hands up and around his neck. "John, please. Talk to me."

For one naked moment, his eyes mirrored the longing she felt. Then he gently disengaged her arms. "Don't make this harder than it has to be."

"But it doesn't have to be hard. That's what I've been trying to tell you. Sure, I want to take the job, but not at the cost of losing you. I'll turn it down."

He stared at her. "No. Don't do that, Sydney. I think you're right. This job offer was probably meant to be. Actually, it's really made things easier for me."

"I . . . I don't understand."

"Look, Sydney, for a while now, I've realized we made a mistake in getting engaged."

If he'd stabbed her through the heart with a knife, her pain wouldn't have been greater.

He continued speaking as if he hadn't just delivered a body blow. "I had already come to the conclusion that it wasn't going to work. I've been trying to think of a way to tell you."

"John . . ." He couldn't mean this. He couldn't!

"So I think we should just say goodbye like two adults and get on with our lives."

Chapter Fourteen

"Goodbye?" Sydney whispered.

His eyes were unreadable. "Yes."

"John, this is crazy! I love you, and I know you love me. Don't try to deny it!"

A muscle twitched in his cheek. He shrugged. "I'll get over it, and you will, too."

"But why should we have to?" she cried, desperation pushing her. She couldn't accept his edict that it was over between them. She didn't know what his motives were for doing what he was doing, but she was sure he wasn't telling her the truth. For whatever reason, he had decided this was the way things had to be. But Sydney loved him too much to just walk away. She'd never walked away from any challenge in her entire life, and she wasn't about to start now. Especially since this challenge was more important than any she'd faced.

He turned away so she couldn't see his eyes. "Our relationship was doomed from the start," he said.

"No! I don't believe that!"

He shrugged. "Whether you choose to believe it or not, you can't change the facts."

"The facts! John, you're twisting everything. The thing I don't understand is *why*."

He finally looked at her again. "The reason you don't understand is that you refuse to see anything you don't want to see. From the very beginning, you've had the idea in your mind that you could change me. You didn't like what I did for a living, so you decided I didn't like it, either. You wanted me to sell my house, and you never gave a thought as to why I couldn't. And now—" He broke off, running his hands through his hair in a gesture of futility. "Oh, what's the use. Like I said, let's just forget it." He smiled cynically. "It was great while it lasted. Can't we just leave it at that?"

Sydney stared at him. Her chest heaved as she fought to control her emotions. When she finally spoke, her voice was as flat and hard as his had been. "Maybe you're right. Maybe I could never have been happy with a coward for a husband."

He flinched.

Good! She'd finally gotten to him. "I thought by now," she continued implacably, "that you'd have finally realized what you're doing to your life and stopped."

"You're talking in riddles."

"All right. I'll speak just as plainly as you have, then. You're afraid, John. Afraid of life. You're hiding in your safe little cocoon, and you're scared to come out. You think as long as you stay in there and take no chances, nothing can hurt you again."

"You don't know what you're talking about." But his face had drained of color.

"I think I do," Sydney said, desperation fueling her words. "Because I was doing the same thing before I met you, John. The difference is, I was hiding from a part of myself. Because I was afraid, too. Afraid of being a woman. Afraid of failure and rejection. You showed me I didn't have to be afraid. You helped me crawl out of my cocoon and face my femininity." She walked toward him and placed her hand on his cheek.

Something flickered in his eyes, and hope spurred Sydney on. "John, please, please don't do this. I love you. And you've admitted that you love me. I don't believe our engagement is a mistake. I think we can build a good life together, if only you'll meet me halfway. I know you want to go back to practicing law. I know you're bored silly by what you're doing. Please, John, face it. Admit it. And come with me to Washington."

His body was rigid as he answered her. "You're the one who's refusing to face the truth."

Sydney sighed. She dropped her hand. It was no use. He refused to see. "Have it your way," she said sadly. "But if you were honest with yourself, you'd admit I'm right."

*   *   *

Sydney made one final plea before walking out the door. She knew she was begging, but so much was at stake, she didn't care.

"Don't throw away what we've found together, John. Please think about what I've said."

They never did eat their dinner.

She finally left. She drove home in a daze, and was surprised to find herself in her parking garage. She didn't remember any part of the trip.

It wasn't until she was unlocking the door to her condo that she realized she was still wearing John's engagement ring.

Sydney's words ate at John.

No matter how many times he told himself she was wrong, that all she'd done was spout psychobabble at him, he couldn't stop thinking about her accusations.

But she *was* wrong.

He wasn't afraid.

He wasn't hiding from life.

Those charges were ridiculous. He was simply trying to give his children something safe and secure. Something they could count on. Something that wouldn't be snatched away from them as their mother had been snatched away from them.

He was building something good and solid. He was safeguarding their future.

Still, Sydney's words refused to go away.

The following week crawled by. Sydney hoped against hope that John would call her.

Wednesday. Thursday. Friday. The weekend.

All went by with no word.

The telephone at home and at the office remained ominously silent.

Finally, on Monday, nearly a week since their confrontation, Sydney knew John wasn't going to change his mind. He wasn't going to call her.

She removed her engagement ring and placed it in its original box. She wrapped the box carefully and asked Norma to send it by express delivery to John. She didn't include a note.

Sydney's engagement ring arrived Tuesday afternoon. John stared at the box when Janet brought it into his office. He knew without opening it what was inside. He could feel Janet's eyes as he pretended nonchalance, placing the box on his desk unopened.

"Aren't you going to open it?" she asked.

"No." He turned back to his computer and pretended to study the screen.

He didn't look up until Janet left his office.

Wednesday morning, first thing, Sydney called Neil Creighton. "I accept your offer," she said.

"Wonderful! I was beginning to worry when I didn't hear from you."

"I'm sorry. I had some things to work out, but they're all settled now."

"Good. If I can help your fiancé find a job in Washington, I'll be glad to do so. What does he do?"

Sydney ignored the sharp stab of pain that suddenly made it hard to breathe. "Thank you, Neil. But that won't be necessary."

"Well, if you should find it is, the offer stands."

"I appreciate that."

"Will you be able to start the first of April?"

"I hope so. I have to talk to our managing partner, but I think the firm will release me by then. After all, that's almost four weeks' notice."

"Good. Let me know. Oh, and when you come to Washington for the awards ceremony, if you want me to, I can have my secretary line up some apartments or townhouses for you to look at. Even if you plan to buy a house, you'll need somewhere to live while you look."

"That's very thoughtful of you."

"Good. Then that's all settled. I'm very pleased, Sydney. Very excited. I think you're going to do a terrific job and lead the league to new heights."

Somehow, Sydney got through the next ten days. For a while there, after she'd sent the ring back to John, she was sure she would hear from him. Finally, as three or four days passed, her hope faded, then died. A dull resignation set in. Even the upcoming trip to Washington and her much-anticipated dinner at the White House didn't lift her spirits.

Two days before she was scheduled to leave for the awards ceremony, her mother called her at the office.

Sydney's heart filled with dread as she picked up her phone. Something terrible must have happened. The one and only time her mother had ever called her at work had been when her father had fallen off a ladder.

"Mom? Is something wrong?"

"No. I was just hoping you could meet me for lunch today."

Sydney hesitated. She hadn't planned to go out to lunch. She was trying to get all of her work caught up so that when she turned her case files over to her successor, they'd be in good order.

"It's very important," her mother said.

They met at Brennan's, and Sydney felt battered by the memories that assailed her when she walked through the door. The last time she'd been to Brennan's had been with John and his children.

Her mother was waiting in the foyer. She smiled when she saw Sydney and walked over. They hugged. Helena Wells looked quietly elegant, as always, in a simple rose wool dress with her mink casually slung over her shoulders.

Once they were seated and had placed their orders, her mother said, "Sydney, I've thought and thought about this for days, and I finally decided I just had to tell you."

Sydney toyed with her water glass and waited.

"Your father has done something very wrong, and I think you need to know about it."

"What?" Sydney said, alarmed now.

"He went to see John. He told John about the job offer from the Children's Advocacy League."

Sydney frowned. "What do you mean? *I* told John about the job."

Her mother spoke slowly. "Before you'd ever had a chance to talk with John, your father went over to John's house and told him about the offer you'd received. He informed John that you were going to turn down the job if John disapproved. He also told him that if you refused the job because of him, you would regret it the rest of your life."

Sydney licked her lips. So that was it. John had been lying when he'd said he'd been thinking about breaking up with her. He'd simply been reacting to her father's pronouncement.

Sydney sighed. She wasn't really surprised. She wasn't even very angry. What her father had done was typical of his modus operandi. When he saw what he perceived to be a stumbling block, he simply removed it. In his eyes, John would be no more than that. A barrier between Sydney and the goals Sid had set for her.

How could Sydney be angry when she'd always known this about her father and loved him, anyway? Still, she couldn't permit this kind of behavior to continue.

"Thanks for telling me, Mom."

Helena sighed. "I love your father, Sydney, but I've never been blind to his faults. Still, what he's done isn't totally his fault. I have to bear some blame in this, too."

"You! You didn't do anything."

"Yes. Yes, I did."

"What did you do?"

"I knew, from the time you were a little girl, that your father was determined to make you into a replica of himself, whether you wanted to be molded that way or not. I knew, yet I did nothing. Even when I saw that you weren't very happy, I still did nothing.'' She reached across the table and grasped Sydney's hand. ''I'm sorry, Sydney. I'm so sorry. I shouldn't have allowed him to take over your life that way. It was wrong. I-I just, I don't know, I took the easy way out. I didn't want to buck your father. I wanted peace, so I sacrificed you.''

''Oh, Mom...'' Sydney felt close to tears. ''It's okay.''

''It's *not* okay. I should have spoken up long ago. You never had a chance.''

''I turned out okay. Didn't I?'' Sydney bit her lip. The tears were very close. Too close. She was going to make a spectacle of herself if she didn't get herself under control.

''You're more than okay,'' her mother said, ''no thanks to me.''

Mother and daughter looked at each other.

''I love you, Sydney. Remember that, will you? I've always loved you and been proud of you, no matter what you did or didn't do. And I always will.''

Sydney cried all the way back to the office. She wasn't sure why she was crying, but for some stupid reason, she couldn't seem to stop.

She pulled into the parking garage and parked her car. Before getting out, she twisted the rearview mirror around so she could see herself.

Omigod, she thought. I can't go inside looking like this.

She started the car again and drove home. When she got there, she called the office. "Norma, something I ate at lunch must have disagreed with me. I don't feel well, so I'm taking the rest of the day off."

"Okay, Miss Wells."

"Tell Mr. Folger, will you?"

"I will."

Sydney washed her face and changed into jeans and a pullover sweater. Then she called her parents' home.

Her father answered. "Hello," he said.

"Dad? It's Sydney."

"How's my girl doing?" he said, all bluff and hearty.

"Dad, we need to talk. Can I come over?"

"Sure, sure. Of course, you can come over. Is something wrong?"

"Let's wait until I get there."

Thirty minutes later, her father ushered her in. "Where's Mom?" Sydney said.

"She went out for lunch, and she hasn't come back yet. Probably shopping, or something. You know your mother."

No, I don't really know her. Not yet, anyway, but I plan to remedy that.

They went into his study, where he promptly removed a cigar from his cigar box. "You don't mind, do you?" he said.

Sydney shook her head.

"So what's this all about?" he asked after he'd lighted the cigar.

"You went to see John, didn't you?"

Surprise flared in his eyes. "What makes you say that?"

"Please, Daddy, don't lie to me. I know you went to see John."

"Did he tell you that?"

"No. He wouldn't. But I know you went, nevertheless." Sydney sighed heavily and sank back into her chair.

Her father smiled sheepishly. "You're not mad at me, are you, baby?"

"No, I'm not mad. But I'm sad." Her gaze met his. "I want to think you went to see him out of love for me, but just once I wish you could love me enough to let me make my own decisions."

"Even when I know that decision would be a terrible mistake?"

"Even then."

She could see he was about to say something else, but he stopped. Their gazes held for a long moment.

"I love John, Daddy," she said softly. "I don't want to lose him." Tears threatened again, but Sydney fought them. "I won't be happy without him."

"But Sydney! What about the job? You've worked all of your life for something like this. You can't give it up."

"Yes, I know. But I can't help thinking that if you hadn't interfered, maybe John and I would have been able to work something out."

Her father got up and came over to her chair. He reached for her hands, pulling her up. He wrapped his arms around her and held her against his chest. "I'm sorry, baby. All I've ever wanted is your happiness."

Sydney knew he thought that's what he wanted, and she guessed that, in the end, that's what mattered. There were all kinds of things she could say to him, all kinds of accusations she could make, but he was her father. And she loved him. She hugged him hard.

"Do you want me to call John?" her father asked. "Maybe I can change his mind. Persuade him to go with you."

"No, Daddy, this is between John and me." Sydney looked up. "But thank you for asking."

Chapter Fifteen

John walked out of Charley's 517 after taking a prospective client to lunch. He stood on the sidewalk for a minute, then turned in the direction of the lot where he'd parked his car.

He walked straight into Lowell Hobbs, an ex-colleague from his days at Chasan & Jeglinski.

"John!" Lowell said, his round face creasing into a smile. "How the hell are ya?" He pumped John's hand enthusiastically.

John grinned. Lowell had always been a favorite of his. "I'm doing great. How about you?"

"Never better. You comin' or goin'?"

"Going."

"Too bad. We coulda had lunch together."

"We'll do it another time. How're Jenny and the kids?"

"Jenny's fine. Pregnant again." He grinned happily.

John laughed. "Don't you know what causes that?"

Lowell's grin expanded. "Say, you still piddlin' around with that temporary agency? When're you coming back to the real world, anyway? Or are you plannin' to play it safe forever?"

Stung, John forced himself to laugh off Lowell's remark. *Keep it light. Don't let him see he got to you.* "Hell, you're just jealous."

Lowell laughed, too. "Yeah, I probably am." Then his face sobered. "Seriously, we miss you, John. We were talking about you just the other day. We agree that you've got too much talent to spend the rest of your life as a salesman. I know the partners would take you back in a minute. Hell, old man Jeglinski said as much. He asks about you all the time."

They talked for a while longer, then Lowell said, "Well, buddy, I'd better let you go. But call me, will ya?"

John was still mulling over Lowell's remarks when he walked into the agency a little later in the day.

Janet looked up. "How'd it go?"

"How'd what go?" He took his telephone messages out of his message slot. He leafed through them absently.

"The lunch with Bruce Pritchard."

He glanced at her. She gave him a quizzical smile. "Oh," he said. "Lunch was fine. I think we'll get his business."

"You don't seem too happy about that."

"Yeah, well." He plopped down in the chair beside her desk and looked at her. "Jan, tell me something—honestly."

"Of course."

"Two people in the last couple of weeks have accused me of hiding out from the world. Do you think that's true?"

She hesitated. Her gaze met his, their dark depths clear and honest. "In a way," she said softly.

John nodded thoughtfully. For a long time they were both silent.

"Who are the two people?" she finally asked.

He shrugged. "Sydney. And Lowell Hobbs. Remember him?"

Janet chuckled. "How could I forget him? Don't you remember? Many moons ago, you and Andrea fixed me up on a blind date with Lowell."

"Oh, yeah. I'd forgotten." They'd both been so sure Lowell and Janet would hit it off, but they hadn't.

"What prompted Sydney and Lowell to say what they did?" Janet asked.

John told her about Sydney's job offer and about their breakup.

"I wondered what had happened," Janet said gently. "I knew *something* must have happened, because you haven't been yourself for days." She reached over and squeezed his hand. "I'm sorry, John."

"I thought you'd be glad."

She frowned. "Why would I be glad?"

"Oh, come on, Jan. You never thought Sydney and I were right for each other."

"Maybe I was wrong."

"My sister? Wrong?" Janet didn't laugh at his feeble attempt at humor.

Instead, she answered thoughtfully. "She made you happy. I didn't want to admit it, but she did."

He nodded and looked away. He didn't want Janet to see the bleakness in his heart.

"Maybe I . . . maybe I was jealous of her, John."

Her words startled him. He looked at her. "Jealous? Why would you be jealous?"

Janet shrugged. "I'm not proud of myself for having these feelings, but I kind of liked taking care of you and the kids. Maybe I just didn't want to think that someone was going to replace me."

"Aw, Jan . . ."

She smiled, but the smile was sad. "Remember that time when you got so mad at me and said I needed a couple of kids to keep me from meddling in your life?"

"That was a low blow. I'm really sorry—"

"No! You were right. That's exactly what I need. And your saying it made me really think about my life and what I want out of it." She absently twisted a paper clip in her fingers. "I've been doing a lot of thinking lately."

Slowly, John said, "If I were to leave the agency, what would you do?"

Janet smiled. "I'd sell the business and go full speed ahead with adopting a child. Maybe a couple of children." She gave him a shy look. "Mike and I have already looked into it. We've found out that if you're willing to take older children, it's not so difficult to adopt."

"Are you saying you wouldn't care if you had to give up the business?"

"That's exactly what I'm saying."

"But starting this business was your idea."

"I know. I just didn't realize how much it would take out of me." Janet sighed. "I'm tired, John. I don't want to work this hard, especially when I never intended to be a career woman."

"But why did you suggest we go into business if you didn't want to?"

"I was feeling frustrated, I guess. I hadn't been able to get pregnant, and then, with Andrea dying and everything... I don't know. It just seemed like a good idea."

For the rest of the day, John reflected upon their conversation. And the next morning, he was still thinking about it when he went downstairs to start his workday.

About ten o'clock, John heard the front doorbell ring, and the *tap, tap, tap* of Janet's high heels as she went to answer it. A few seconds later, she walked back to his office.

"Delivery for you," she said, handing him a red, white and blue flat cardboard envelope.

"Thanks."

He opened the envelope absently, fully expecting it to be tax forms from his accountant. When he removed the airline tickets, he stared at them uncomprehendingly.

There was a note attached. It read:

> The flight to Washington leaves at two o'clock tomorrow. Please come.

He had forgotten that Sydney had ordered their tickets a month ago. He had also forgotten that tomorrow was the day they were scheduled to leave for the awards ceremony.

He stared at the tickets for a long time.

He wasn't coming.

On a day that should have been one of the happiest of her life, Sydney stared out the window at her gate and thought about how different things could have been. The sky was leaden, a perfect match for her leaden heart. It was raining, a light, drizzly rain that promised to continue all day.

She sighed.

Down below, men in uniforms scurried about. A food truck was parked alongside the big silver jet, and she knew the meals for her flight were being unloaded and stored in the galley.

She looked at her watch. One twenty-eight. They would board soon.

He wasn't coming.

She had hoped, she had prayed, she had bargained with God. None of it had done any good.

John wasn't coming.

Face it. You're not going to see him again.

She bit her bottom lip. Oh, God, why did life have to be so hard? Why couldn't things work out the way they were supposed to?

She closed her eyes. *I love you, John. I love you.* She tried to communicate her thoughts across the miles that separated them.

"We will begin boarding flight 453 for Washington National in a few minutes. Will passengers with small children and those passengers who need assistance please come to the gate?"

Sydney turned away from the window and walked listlessly back to her seat. She sank onto it. Across from her, a pair of young lovers whispered together. The boy—God, he couldn't be more than nineteen— had his arm around the girl. He nuzzled her ear, and she giggled. The boy was dressed in a naval uniform. Sydney wondered if he was a student at the naval academy.

Their joy in each other pierced Sydney's heart. She and John had been like that at one time.

John, John. Why? Why does it have to be this way?

How was she ever going to forget him? Even the thought of her commendation, the dinner at the White House and the exciting new job ahead of her, didn't make her feel happy. There was an aching emptiness inside of her, and she was desperately afraid it would never be filled.

"First-class passengers can board at any time," the gate attendant announced, startling Sydney. "And now, would those passengers seated in rows sixteen through thirty-five please come forward and begin boarding?''

Sydney remained seated. She was flying first-class, but she didn't feel like getting on the plane yet. If John were here, she'd be eager to get on. Eager to take off. Eager to reach her destination.

He's not coming.

The couple across from her stood. The boy gathered the girl close, and they kissed. Once. Twice. Long passionate kisses. They held each other tightly.

Sydney's eyes filled with tears. She looked away. *John. John.* Her heart actually hurt, with a sharp, physical pain that made it hard to breathe.

"Goodbye, Billy," the girl said. "Write to me. Call me."

The boy grinned. Lipstick was smeared on his mouth, and his eyes seemed dazed. They kissed again. Then, as the girl's face crumpled and she groped for a tissue to wipe the tears that streamed down her face, he waved sheepishly and grabbed up his duffel bag. He loped off toward the gate and disappeared into the jetway.

Sydney looked at the girl, who was crying in earnest now. For one moment, their gazes met. The girl turned away, her shoulders sagging with unhappiness.

Sydney knew exactly how the girl felt and wished she had the luxury of expressing her emotions so openly.

And then the girl walked toward the window and stood with her face pressed against the pane. Sydney knew she'd be standing there long after the plane had taxied out to the runway.

A few minutes later, the gate attendant picked up her hand mike and said, "All passengers sitting in rows one through fifteen may board at this time."

The rest of the waiting passengers surged forward. Sydney picked up her carry-on bag and walked slowly to the gate. She was in no hurry. Her seat would still be there, no matter when she boarded.

She looked at her watch again. One forty-two.

At 1:47, she was securely tucked into her window seat in the first-class section. The wide leather seat was comfortable, but it didn't matter. Nothing mattered. Only John, and he wasn't coming.

She looked at the empty seat beside her.

Empty.

What an awful-sounding word. It was ugly. Stark and ugly.

Empty.

Who had ever coined that word, anyway?

Sydney turned away from the sight of the seat. She stared out the window.

Around her, she could hear the noises of passengers continuing to board, the flight attendants in the galley, the revving and testing of the engines.

"Would you like a cocktail, Miss Wells?"

Sydney looked up.

The friendly green eyes of a flight attendant greeted her. Sydney's gaze dropped to the name tag the woman wore. *Shelley.* "No, thank you," Sydney said. "Maybe later."

"All right. Just let me know. What about a magazine? Or a pillow and blanket?"

"Nothing." *Just go away. Cocktails and magazines aren't what I need. Pillows and blankets aren't what I need.*

Sydney closed her eyes. She heard the *thump, thump* of overhead bins closing. The rattle of dishes and utensils as the rest of the equipment was stored. The myriad other noises as passengers settled down and the remaining luggage was stowed. Then the almost imperceptible motion as the plane began to back away from the jetway.

Then she heard the distinctive *click* of the seat belt closing in the seat beside her.

Sydney's eyes snapped open and she turned.

John smiled at her. "I suppose you thought you were rid of me," he said lightly.

"John." Shock and delight cascaded in her mind. Her heart seemed permanently lodged in her throat.

"Is that all you can say, Counselor?" His smile expanded into a grin, and his warm brown eyes sparkled. "What happened to that silver tongue of yours?"

He took her hand, and his smile faded as they looked at each other.

She curled her fingers around his. Her heart was thumping like a piston now, and she could feel tears welling up in her eyes. "John," she whispered. She felt incapable of saying anything more.

He leaned over and kissed her, his warm mouth lingering against hers. "You'll never be rid of me, Sydney. From now on, we're stuck together like glue."

Then he kissed her again. When the kiss ended, he smiled down into her eyes.

Her heart was so full, she wasn't sure she could speak. Finally, she said, "Does this mean you ... and the kids ... are moving to Washington with me?"

"If you still want us."

"Oh, John." The tears fell in earnest now. "Damn," she said, swiping at them. "I'm like a damned waterworks lately."

John pulled a handkerchief out of his pocket. He wiped away her tears. "You were right," he said. "I was hiding. But no more. Never again." He leaned close. "I love you, Sydney."

"Oh, I love you, too, John. And I'm so happy you're here. I was so sad. So afraid I'd never see you again."

"I was pretty miserable, too."

"What about the kids? Have you told them about Washington?"

"Not yet. I thought we'd do that together."

"Do you think they'll mind?"

"Maybe at first. But in the end, Emily will be excited. She loves challenges." He smiled. "She's a lot like you."

A wonderful feeling of warmth slid through Sydney.

"And Jeffrey, well, he's little. He'll adjust fast." His hand tightened around hers. "I've already called a couple of people in Washington. I've got some feelers out for jobs."

The plane had reached the runway, and the pilot said, "Flight attendants, be seated for takeoff."

They were silent as the plane barreled down the runway, then John reached into his jacket pocket. "You forgot something." He opened the velvet jeweler's box and removed her engagement ring. Taking her hand again, he slipped it on. "Don't take it off again." But he smiled when he said it.

"I won't."

As the plane lifted off, Sydney's heart soared along with it. She knew the future would always be uncertain, because no one could predict what would happen. She also knew there would be other problems along the way, but together, she and John would face them and surmount them.

The plane climbed and banked, then climbed again.

John squeezed her hand. "I love you," he mouthed.

"I love you."

They held hands tightly as the plane broke through the clouds, and golden sunshine, filled with the promise of the days to come, flooded the windows.

*   *   *   *   *

Silhouette

SPECIAL EDITION™

COMING NEXT MONTH

#925 FOR THE BABY'S SAKE—Christine Rimmer
That Special Woman!
Andrea McCreary had decided to raise her unborn baby on her own.
Clay Barrett had generously offered a proposal of marriage, and soon
realized their arrangement would not be without passion....

#926 C IS FOR COWBOY—Lisa Jackson
Love Letters
Only the promise of a reward convinced Sloan Redhawk to rescue
headstrong, spoiled Casey McKee. He despised women like her—yet
once he rescued her, he was unable to let her go!

#927 ONE STEP AWAY—Sherryl Woods
Only one thing was missing from Ken Hutchinson's life: the woman of
his dreams. Now he'd found Beth Callahan, but convincing her to join
his ready-made family wouldn't be so easy....

#928 ONLY ST. NICK KNEW—Nikki Benjamin
Alison Kent was eager to escape the holiday hustle and bustle. Meeting
Frank Bradford—and his adorable twin sons—suddenly showed her this
could indeed be the most wonderful time of the year!

#929 JAKE RYKER'S BACK IN TOWN—Jennifer Mikels
Hellion Jake Ryker had stormed out of town, leaving behind a broken
heart. Stunned to discover he had returned, Leigh McCall struggled with
stormy memories—and with Jake's renewed passionate presence.

#930 ABIGAIL AND MISTLETOE—Karen Rose Smith
Abigail Fox's generous nature never allowed her to think of herself.
Her heart needed the kind of mending only Brady Crawford could
provide—and their kiss under the mistletoe was just the beginning....

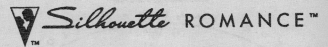

Silhouette ROMANCE™

'Tis the season for romantic bliss.
It all begins with just one kiss—

UNDER THE MISTLETOE

Celebrate the joy of the season and the thrill of romance with this special collection:

#1048 ANYTHING FOR DANNY by Carla Cassidy—Fabulous Fathers
#1049 TO WED AT CHRISTMAS by Helen R. Myers
#1050 MISS SCROOGE by Toni Collins
#1051 BELIEVING IN MIRACLES by Linda Varner—Mr. Right, Inc.
#1052 A COWBOY FOR CHRISTMAS by Stella Bagwell
#1053 SURPRISE PACKAGE by Lynn Bulock

Available in December, from Silhouette Romance.

SRXMAS

JINGLE BELLS, WEDDING BELLS:
Silhouette's Christmas Collection for 1994

Christmas Wish List

*To beat the crowds at the malls and get the perfect present for *everyone,* even that snoopy Mrs. Smith next door!

*To get through the holiday parties without running my panty hose.

*To bake cookies, decorate the house and serve the perfect Christmas dinner—just like the women in all those magazines.

*To sit down, curl up and read my Silhouette Christmas stories!

Join *New York Times* bestselling author Nora Roberts, along with popular writers Barbara Boswell, Myrna Temte and Elizabeth August, as we celebrate the joys of Christmas—and the magic of marriage—with

JINGLE
BELLS,
WEDDING
BELLS

Silhouette's Christmas Collection for 1994.

JBWB

**Another wonderful year of romance
concludes with**

Christmas
Memories

Share in the magic and memories of romance
during the holiday season with this collection of two
full-length contemporary Christmas stories,
by two bestselling authors

**Diana Palmer
Marilyn Pappano**

Available in December at your favorite retail outlet.

Only from

Silhouette®

™

where passion lives.

XMMEM